Dι

The Trials of the Tredgolds

Vol. 3

SALZWASSER
VERLAG

Dutton Cook

The Trials of the Tredgolds

Vol. 3

Reprint of the original, first published in 1864.

1st Edition 2022 | ISBN: 978-3-75259-536-9

Verlag (Publisher): Salzwasser Verlag GmbH, Zeilweg 44, 60439 Frankfurt, Deutschland
Vertretungsberechtigt (Authorized to represent): E. Roepke, Zeilweg 44, 60439 Frankfurt, Deutschland
Druck (Print): Books on Demand GmbH, In de Tarpen 42, 22848 Norderstedt, Deutschland

THE TRIALS OF THE TREDGOLDS.

THE

TRIALS OF THE TREDGOLDS.

A Novel.

BY DUTTON COOK

IN THREE VOLUMES.

VOL. III.

Second Edition.

LONDON

1864.

CONTENTS.

CHAPTER VIII.

CHAPTER IX.

CHAPTER X.

CHAPTER XI.

CHAPTER XII.

CHAPTER XIII.

THE TRIALS OF THE TREDGOLDS.

CHAPTER I.

"IT CANNOT BE."

It must be confessed that Herbert Gifford received not very gracefully or gratefully Clare's expressions of sympathy. He listened in a sullen, gloomy way, waiting until she had finished, and appeared at last to be rather more bored than comforted. It was not that he had any doubt of the genuineness of Clare's kind efforts to console him, or suspected any ridicule to be lying *perdu* in her gentle words and tender actions. He knew well that she was not "teasing him" this time; but he was conscious that he was not being treated according to his deserts; that he did not merit such kindly regard; and he shrunk from it, guilty and ashamed. He was aware that Clare proceeded upon the assumption that he had been true to his word; that he had made a sacrifice of his affections; had given up Liz at his father's bidding; and was acutely suffering in consequence. But this was not strictly the case. He had persuaded himself that by the spirit, if not by the letter of his promise to his father, a last interview with Liz was permitted to him; and after this a further last word in a fervid letter, taking an eternal adieu of her. But by some means, he scarcely understood how, these had led to additional meetings, to renewed correspondence. As in the case of a favourite actor reluctantly taking leave of the scene of his triumphs, there was a long series of farewells. It was so hard to say good-bye, and keep to it, that the lovers said the word a thousand times, and didn't keep to it. What Mr. Gifford, senior, had stigmatized as a disgraceful connection was therefore, in point of fact, maintained with not less vitality than before. False to his father, Herbert was true to Liz. But it is due to him to say that he was very miserable. He was fairly frightened at the error of his conduct. Yet he had not sufficient strength of mind to remedy this by change. He could not abandon Liz—perhaps, for one reason because she possessed great influence over him, and would not let him.

Pains and precautions were taken to prevent the discovery of their love. Liz's letters no longer came to Cumberland Crescent; they were directed to a post-office in Oxford Street, and were called for regularly by Herbert himself. His despatches to Liz were not addressed to her father's house, but to the care of "a lady friend," an affectionate dressmaker in the neighbourhood of Whitfield Street, in whose discretion and trustworthiness—so Liz assured her lover—implicit reliance might always be placed. And their correspondenco pre-arranged their meetings, which took place, as a rule, in Fitzroy Square, at eight o'clock in the evening. They promenaded round and round that silent, deserted, iron-railinged enclosure for some hours, with unwearying constancy and fortitude. They were engrossed in each other; observation did not disturb them; the cats were not afraid of them; and the policeman blandly tolerated, if he did not absolutely approve and sanction, their proceedings.

Round and round the enclosure, heedless of the weather. If it rained, the trees were there as though expressly to shelter them; or beneath the dome of an umbrella they could dispose themselves with secure compactness. Slowly round and round, with a slight pause perhaps under the gas-lamps, that Herbert might lingeringly study the round splendour of Liz's eyes, and the unutterable love gleaming in them.

Herbert was rather a melancholy and desponding kind of lover. As some people take a sort of sad pleasure in being hopeless invalids, so Herbert seemed inclined to enjoy and to harp upon the miserable side of his situation. He confided to Liz peevish complaints of his father's cruelty; lamented over the suffering to which they were therefore subjected; was without faith in the future; looked forward to no change in their present wretchedness; and asked, with querulous iteration, What were they to do? What was to become of them? He was for ever wounding himself and the lady with these troublesome inquiries. Liz consoled him when she could, lending him some of her superabundant trust in the chapter of accidents. When he was too unreasonable or too despairing to listen to her, she had presence of mind to lean heavily on his arm and weep copiously. By this course the *onus* of consolation was shifted, or at least the attention of her lover was diverted to a nearer trouble. He had to dry her eyes; to busy himself with new assurances of his changeless affection; to girdle her with his arm, the better to support her; and to kiss her back to composure. And this was quite sufficient to occupy him for some little time.

"I don't suppose any fellow ever had such a strict governor as I've got," the young man would groan.

"My poor pet," Liz would coo, affectionately squeezing his arm, as though to remind him there were compensations for his misfortune in her presence, and in her regard for him.

"He gets worse and worse; he's so horribly suspicious; and he's growing so stingy, too, there's no getting a cheque out of him any how now."

"Never mind, dearest; things will change for the better soon, be sure they will."

"I don't see how, Liz. I'm the most wretched beggar living, I do believe."

"How can you say that, you naughty boy?" An arch flashing of her eyes, further squeezing of his arm, and a leaning of her head upon his shoulder. Surely now he must be quite aware of her presence.

"When we're married, Herbert, you know,

we shall look back at all these vexations only to laugh at them," Liz would resume presently.

"Yes, *when*; but I'm sure I don't see my way to getting married; I wish I could."

"I believe I've heard that marriages can be managed very easily and quietly at the registrar's. At least I remember I heard Miss Minns" (the dressmaker) "say so quite promiscuously one day." (Truth to say, Liz had had much converse with her "lady friend" on the subject of Herbert's affection, and the probabilities of speedy union with him.)

"But think of the governor, Liz. He'd be sure to find it out in time; we couldn't expect to keep him always in the dark about it; and what a terrible way he'd be in!"

Liz was silenced; not convinced, however.

"It's a most unfortunate business. Sometimes I almost wish I had never seen you, Liz. I'm the most miserable beggar living, I am. No one would believe the amount of wretchedness I've endured about this affair. And for what good? Heaven only knows how it's all to end."

Liz burst into tears.

"You don't love me, sir; that's what you mean. You're tired of me. It's to me you owe all this trouble. I know it is. You said as much yourself just now. Oh, Herbert, how cruel of you—how wicked! I wouldn't have believed it of you."

"My dearest Liz——"

"No, I'm not. You know I'm not. You love some other woman, you faithless, treacherous boy, you; some woman of rank, and wealth, and beauty, no doubt. But you'll never be loved as you've been by poor simple little me; you never will."

"Indeed, indeed, my darling——"

"You don't love me a bit."

And it was only with much difficulty, great persuading, and abundant demonstration of his tenderness, that she could be induced to renew her trust in him. She was still excited.

"Haven't *I* suffered?" she asked, with some passion. "Has it been all on your side? Have *I* made no sacrifices for you, you naughty, selfish boy? Didn't I give up everything and everybody for your sake? Couldn't I have been married and settled long ago, but for you? Didn't I disappoint my own cousin for you, Herbert? Wasn't he pressing me day after day to go to church with him?" (This wasn't, perhaps, quite the truth; still it was in a measure, and near enough for the occasion.) "Hasn't poor father been thrown out of bread and lost his situation along of you, Herbert? Ain't we all ruined? And now to be told that you don't love me!"

"No, no, Liz."

And much of the work of composing her had to be gone through again. And then protestations of mutual affection had to be again interchanged, and the feasibility of marriage before the registrar—in favour of which course the opinion of Miss Minns, the dressmaker, Liz's "lady friend," had again to be cited—was once more to be brought on for discussion.

The meetings in Fitzroy Square were often conducted on some such plan as that we have endeavoured to bring before the reader.

It had not been possible to conceal from Liz, always watchful, cunning, and curious, the fact that William Moyle's connection with the house of Fordyce and Fordyce had been finally closed. A day or two after his angry scene with Mr. Gifford, the old man found it expedient to furnish his daughter with some particulars of what had happened; to give some explanation of his presence in the house during business-hours. He did this in as few words as possible, timidly and nervously, after his manner; but Liz was quick to understand that her father's quarrel had reference to the proceedings of Herbert and herself. It was not deemed desirable to inform old Zachary of the important change that had taken place in his son's position; it was thought that it would be too great a shock to him to learn that Fordyce and Fordyce had dismissed their old clerk after a prolonged period of service. He was left, therefore, to form his own conclusions; and if, as he sat huddled over the kitchen-fire, carefully supervised and tended by Nance, he missed the sight of his son's legs passing the area-railings on the journey to and fro the City, he was permitted to account for a fact so extraordinary in his own way, and without assistance from any other members of the household.

Mr. Stap had not lately shown himself in Whitfield Street. Possibly he considered it prudent—knowing that William Moyle had now no reasons for leaving his own house to spend the day in the City, and that he would have to be encountered by any visitor to the house—to wait a little, until there was a chance of the old man's wrath subsiding. Meanwhile he had written to Liz to assure her of his fidelity, and had received a reply, affectionately worded, but withholding all information touching the state of affairs in Whitfield Street, with no mention of Herbert Gifford or of her father.

It is fair to say that Liz had some misgivings, not so much as to the propriety, but as to the prudence of her conduct. Her vanity was flattered by the attentions of her two lovers. On that account she would regard with regret the dismissal of either of them; yet that the affair must end in that way at some time or other was clear to her. Which, then, was to be sacrificed? To which of them was she to yield her hand? Of the two, perhaps, she preferred Mr. Stap; not that she was capable of entertaining much real love for him; but he amused her, while Herbert as certainly bored her. Yet Herbert would be rich. There could hardly be a doubt of that; and she set great store upon money. To have plenty; to lead a life of luxury and ease, and indolence, splendidly dressed; to be a fine lady; to loll in a barouche, with rings on her fingers; to appear at the opera in a decidedly low dress, edged with real lace, with flowers in her perfumed hair and diamonds round her superb throat—all this seemed very delightful to her, very precious, and surely within her reach if she became Herbert's wife. As Mrs. Stap, how much less inviting a career was opened to her! Yet she doubted; and tried to obtain assistance from her father in arriving at a decision. But it was with difficulty always that William Moyle could be brought to speak upon the subject.

"I suppose it's quite certain," she said to him one day, "that Herbert will be very rich, isn't it? There can be no doubt about it, I should think."

"His father's very rich," the old man answered slowly; "not so rich as he has been; for things have been bad in the City, and the firm has been a good deal tried lately."

"But Herbert—"

"He's his father's only son. He'll have everything. And he'll be taken into the firm before long, I should say."

"But if he married against his father's wish——"

"I don't see that it could make much difference in the long run."

"But he's very poor now; he told me so himself."

"Perhaps so. His father don't like parting with his money, I dare say."

"He couldn't marry without money."

"It wouldn't be difficult to borrow it, I should think," William Moyle said, with a curious laugh.

"Upon a few pieces of paper with the firm's name at the bottom of them he could raise pretty much what he liked."

"You mean——"

And Liz coloured.

"Never mind what I mean, my girl," said the old man, turning away.

"He's not a member of the firm yet. He's not entitled to——"

"Never mind what he's not entitled to." And then, only half audibly, he went on: "It would be a little beforehand, that's all. It would only be anticipating a little. I don't see that any harm could come it. There's a deal done in very queer paper in the City—queerer than this would be, by long odds—and no one ever a bit the worse. His father wouldn't like it, perhaps," he chuckled; "but what could he do against his own son?"

Whether he intended Liz to hear anything of these remarks, was not clear. She did hear much of what he said, and she began asking herself, Was he sober? Had she rightly understood him? Did he really mean what he said?

"I know nothing about business matters," she said aloud.

And the subject was allowed to drop.

Herbert and his father had not been on very friendly terms since their discussion of the correspondence with Liz Moyle, and Herbert's promise that the "disgraceful connection" should be altogether given up. The young man was inclined to shrink from meeting his father, dreading, perhaps, lest the conversation should be recommenced, and satisfied very likely that his conduct would not by any means bear examination or comment. Mr. Gifford's manner to his son meanwhile was characterized by a scrupulous politeness, that was not without a certain air of irony very annoying to the young man. He had exhausted his allowance, but he saw little chance of obtaining a further supply. His father, he knew, was in no mood to bestow upon him supplementary cheques. And his creditors were pressing him; and he had incurred certain play-debts—especially with Clement Buckhurst—which of course must be paid, if only because Clement was so generously forbearing about them. Strictly speaking, they should have been discharged on the instant; but Clem had very kindly entreated him not to inconvenience himself in any way. So that there was really the more reason why he should not encroach upon kindness so absolutely disinterested.

Herbert was certainly not happy. There seemed to him quite a combination of circumstances to distress him. His pecuniary embarrassments; his unfortunate love affair; his sense of shame at the deceit he had practised; his inability to discover any happy issue out of all these annoyances; and the fact of their all coming upon him simultaneously, brought him wretched days and sleepless nights. He grew irritable and peevish; in his weakness and irresolution he knew not which way to turn—felt often prompted to sit down and cry over his troubles, like a thwarted child. Sometimes he felt tempted to abscond from his father's house altogether, to go anywhere away from his distresses; but such a course required rather more strength of will and fixity of purpose than, unassisted, he could bring to bear upon the occasion. And now, by way of additional aggravation, his father requested his more regular attendance at the offices of Messrs. Fordyce and Fordyce; the secession of William Moyle had left the firm short of hands, and apparently there was much to be done just then. Mr. Gifford was working day and night; he brought books and papers home with him from the City, and took them with him to his study immediately on the conclusion of dinner. He left Cumberland Crescent for his office at an earlier hour in the morning than usual. He grew pale and anxious; many men said, with William Moyle, that things were queer in the City. There was a certain heaviness in the commercial atmosphere that seemed to indicate a coming storm, of which the first few drops had fallen already. One or two houses had stopped payment (but then, after all, no great stress was to be laid upon this fact, because the houses were Greek, and Greek houses have a sort of faculty for stopping payment upon light provocation, as every one knows); and it behoved men to see to their affairs, and merchant-princes to take care that their coronets did not topple from their heads. To Herbert's thinking, this period of commercial difficulty had occurred expressly to visit him with increased vexation.

Clement Buckhurst, as he confessed to himself, could not very well afford to postpone the receipt of the amounts due to him, was quite as much in want of money as anybody else in the world.

"I don't know why I'm so patient with that young cub," he said, speaking of his friend and schoolfellow Herbert Gifford; "I've let him off deuced easy, I know that. Very few fellows could have resisted the temptation of cleaning him out long before this; but I've been no end of tender with him. I suppose it's to please *her*. She'd be very sorry if he came to grief; and if it was through me, I don't think she'd be in a hurry to forgive me. Still, if I'm owed money, I must be paid like anybody else."

And altogether Clement Buckhurst was not very well satisfied. He considered himself in the light of a loser by reason of his leniency in the case of Herbert; and he began to perceive that the chances of his obtaining the hand of Clare Gray were not on the increase as time rolled on. He could not conceal from himself the fact that his advances had not been of late very favourably received. He made no way: his endeavours to assume the position of an accepted lover had not been remarkably successful. His attempts to please were not greatly regarded; he found himself often listened to with indifference, if not with inattention. He found it difficult now even to win a smile, or a bright glance, in return for the pleasant inanities and agreeable nothings in the insinuating utterance of which he was so accomplished a master. Indeed, it is possible that the gentleman had not fully comprehended the limits of his powers of pleasing. These were considerable, but they were not enduring; they would succeed in a brilliant, dashing charge, but they were not calculated for siege purposes; they were so weakened by time. At first Clem—he was so handsome and courtly, so glib, so elegant, with such an air of refinement—charmed very greatly; but he had no reserves to bring into the field after the first effect of his assault had worn off a little, and any sort of resistance to him, if persevered in, would secure his defeat in the long run. Clare had not accepted his suit, and became each day less and less inclined to do so. She could not bring herself to regard him as her affianced husband; sought to prevent his ever thinking of himself in such a light. She stopped him when he ventured to mention anything of his hopes in this respect; and when he tried to assume a lover's privilege of presenting her with necklaces and bracelets (obtained, of course, on credit from his mother's jeweller), she declined to receive them, or anything beyond the trivial offerings that friendship might fairly make, in the way of bouquets, music, etc. She persisted in regarding him as a friend, not as a lover. He was dissatisfied, but he did not despair. He was young and handsome, you see, and had had such small experience of failure.

Women had hitherto smiled upon him so kindly, that he was rather spoiled.

He began to understand, however, that it was time something should be done.

"I've frittered away a whole season," he said, "and I'm pretty much where I began. It won't do at all."

"I'm afraid you've been making an infernal ass of yourself, Clem," his uncle the Honourable Alfred stated frankly.

"I don't consider I'm done yet." But he bit his nails, with not a very hopeful look in his eyes. "If I am, it will be an awful sell."

"Young men," said the Colonel, sententiously, "are very wise now-a-days; but they break down on the woman question. Precocity will do a good deal on a smooth course; but over heavy ground it will always run a very bad second to Experience. Your young fellows of the present day may be doosed knowing, and quick, and clever, and all that; but put them down by a woman, and I never knew one of them that didn't turn out rather a fool than not. It's no use being wide awake if you don't look out in the right direction. And, by Gad, when you've got to do with a woman, you must look out all around you, and pretty sharply too. You're shrewd,

Clem; and you *do* know a thing or two, I allow; but I think this little Gray girl—that's her name, isn't it?—has been one too many for you. Take my advice; never again play a waiting game with a woman; it's time thrown away; it's giving odds against yourself. It's just *time* she most wants; that she may find out how to throw you, and proceed accordingly. But go on with a rush, as you would at a bull or a madman, and the chances are ten to one in your favour. They can't stand impulse, sir, take my word for it; it's infectious, and they're carried away by it. There's some stuff talked about the woman who deliberates being lost; it's infernal rubbish, sir. The woman who deliberates—throws you over."

"Have a cheroot?" says Clem, not very graciously, but as though he thought that, by putting something in the veteran's mouth, he might stop his talking.

It didn't have that effect, however; so Clem tried not to listen, pondering the while what would be the best course for him to adopt.

A few days after this conversation, the uncle and the nephew met again. The Honourable Alfred burst into the young man's rooms in Jasmin Street, and found him as usual dallying with his breakfast.

"I've bad news for you, Clem," the Colonel said solemnly,—"most infernal bad news. I've just got a letter from Hawker—you know Hawker? —General Hawker, an old brother-officer of mine; served in Scinde, under Napier. He writes from Paris. He tells me he met the Beauflowers the other day. He says Beauflower looks frightfully bad, but that his wife is——"

And he stooped down to whisper in the ear of the young man some interesting particulars concerning the condition of Lady Beauflower.

Clement scowled angrily, pushing the breakfast-things away from him.

"You know, my dear Clem, that if it should be a boy—," and the Colonel stopped, with an ominous look; presently he continued,—"there will be the devil and all to pay, indeed there will."

Still Clement said nothing.

"You'll have all the hounds coming upon you with a rush. You must make up your mind what you'll do. It's a very good time for getting away just now. I think of starting for Baden almost immediately myself, after I've dropped round at my agent's to see how my account stands. London in the dog-days is very trying to a man of my bulk, and I can't stand it. I'm getting very fleshy, and I've had rather a swimming in my head lately. It's quite time I go out of Town. You must take care of yourself, Clem, indeed you must; you must really look after your own interests."

"I'll speak to her at once—this afternoon," he said, half audibly.

And he did speak to her. He found her sauntering in the enclosure in front of the house in Cumberland Crescent. He gently pressed her for an answer to his suit, and was—rejected.

"It cannot be, Clement," she said gently, in rather a pained voice.

"You don't mean, Clare dearest"—he urged.

"Indeed, Clement, it cannot be. I am very sorry. Pray don't think harshly of me. Forgive me that I did not, as I should have done, make all this clear to you before—when you first spoke to me. But I could not. I hardly knew what I said or did."

"But, Clare——"

"Indeed, Clement, it cannot be. Pray let us say no more upon this subject. I am very sorry. Believe me, I have real sympathy for you. Let us part for a time. By and by, when all this is over, you will think differently of me. It will not pain you to see me, and we can meet as friends once more."

It was very tenderly, touchingly spoken, with tears in her eyes, and the most silvery plaintiveness in her voice; her hand moved towards him a little way—for him to clasp it, if he would, as a friend.

What more could she do? She could not tell him that she had once loved him, almost, for ten days or so; and that then, somehow, her tenderness for him had faded away, because there was not sufficient worth in him for it to get secure hold of, possibly; and that then she had wearied of him, wondering a little at herself the while.

"If you knew how I love you, Clare!"

She turned away—not impatiently. Perhaps she felt she ought to bear some punishment; but undoubtedly his persistence grieved her—did not assist him. He saw this himself at last, and grew angry.

"Is it because you love some one else?" he asked, rather rudely, with a sneer.

"You have no right to speak to me like that, Clement," she said gently, yet with some stateliness of manner.

He was sorry in a moment. He recovered himself, and took leave of her with calm grace, taking her hand into his, pressing it ever so slightly, as he said,

"Good-bye."

"Poor Clement!" This was when he had gone.

She looked pale and sad, and the tears clustered thickly upon her long eyelashes.

Clement rejoined his uncle.

"Tricked, jilted, flung over!" he cried, in a furious rage. "I should like to know who has stepped in between her and me!" and he fell to calling her names,—not very choice ones, some of them. "Some one else has got hold of her. But I'll have revenge, I will, I will" (and here he swore stoutly). "I won't be tricked in this way. I'll be revenged upon her, upon that fool Herbert, upon her father, upon some one; I will, by——"

"Don't make an idiot of yourself, Clem," his uncle interrupted him, quite calmly.

He blew a great cloud from his cheroot, and surveyed his nephew carefully through the smoke, as though he could see him better in that way; just as men find they can study the sun more advantageously for regarding it through a dimmed glass.

CHAPTER II.

DISINTERESTEDNESS.

"REVENGE is rubbish," said the Honourable Alfred, heartily, in his profoundest bass voice. There would seem to be something of a Christian savour about the sentence; but it is probable that the veteran arrived at his conclusion by rather a pagan process of thought. "I never knew revenge do any man any good. It's mere waste of time. I thought you were above talking such nonsense, Clem; that you knew better than to be going on like a man in a play. Now-a-days, if anything happens to you that you don't like, why, you have to grin and bear it as well as you can; and I'm not sure that it isn't a good plan. It's not pleasant; but it's very safe. Formerly, of course, it was different. If you felt aggrieved, why, you called your man out, and winged him if you could, or got winged yourself, just as it might happen. I've been out myself more than once. My affair with Grimstone of the Buffs was in '18 or '19; or was it in '20? I forget the precise year; but it's of no consequence. I hit him in the knee. We were very good friends afterwards; but of course he was lamed for life. Nobody goes to Wimbledon or Wormwood Scrubbs in these times, however, and no one ever did go for revenge particularly; but much more because it was a social and proper sort of thing to do,—a gentlemanly method of settling a difference of opinion. However, you can't call a man out now whatever he does: unless you want to be chaffed in all the papers and caricatured in *Punch*. You must go about and pretend not to mind; and by dint of long pretending you don't care, you won't really care a bit in time. And then, you know, in this case there's no one to fight; you can't call out the City gent just because his stepdaughter's thrown you over; nor his son either; it's quite absurd. This isn't the sort of thing to be settled in that way. You must get the whole thing out of your head, Clem, as quick as you can. You'll be better after dinner, if you are careful about your wine. Things always do seem ever so much worse before dinner."

"I won't stand it; by Heaven, I won't! I'll

pay her out for this somehow or other," Clem cried savagely.

"Drop it, Clem; drop it. It's absurd. You can't talk of a woman in that sort of way, you know; it won't do at all."

"I won't be treated like this by man or woman. I'll let her know who she's got to deal with. I'm not a pitiful fool like that Herbert Gifford, to be wound round her finger, and unwound again, just as she may please. I'll teach her to trick me, the jilt!"

It will be noted that Clem Buckhurst was less courtly and refined out of Clare's presence than in it; but then he is not the only man whose conduct varies considerably according to the society in which he finds himself. Indeed, some of the most delicate specimens of the dainty class known as "ladies' men" have been known to demean themselves not very nicely when removed from the influence of feminine looks and smiles, and relieved from the necessity of picking and choosing their phrases, and bringing only their prettiest thoughts to the surface. And then, in addition, it must be borne in mind that Clem had been from his cradle a spoilt child, pampered and cossetted in every way; and the notion of being crossed and thwarted made him furious, vindictive, and ungentlemanly even. He had lost his languid ease of manner; he was rocking to and fro, swinging about his limbs, petulantly disquiet. His uncle watched him with sorrowful surprise. He had overrated Clem's man-of-the-world wisdom; he had only seen him in comparatively fair weather; unquestionably he did not appear at all to advantage in a storm. He was beating about, apparently, without rudder or compass; and in his anger he looked almost ugly."

"Be reasonable, Clem, my dear boy; be reasonable," said his uncle gently.

"So I am reasonable, as she shall find. It isn't likely I could bear to be tricked like this, without saying a word, without resenting it. I've been made a fool of."

"You must remember that you gave me to understand some time ago that there was a degree of uncertainty about the issue of the affair."

"If I did, it wasn't because I really thought so. Haven't I been encouraged by her mother—by her stepfather? Wasn't Gifford always asking me to the house? Wasn't it looked upon as a settled thing by everybody? And yet she allowed me to go on to the end, without the least hint of her intention to disappoint me; without one effort to spare me the mortification of rejection." This was not quite correct, but he was too wrathful to be particular about such a small matter as truth. "It's deuced hard; and I feel it, I can tell you. And I won't be beaten; I won't give in yet. I'll see Gifford about it; by heaven, I will! I'll hear what he's got to say about it. Perhaps he can bring her to her senses."

"No, no, Clem, my dear boy; drop it, drop it. Take my advice. What *is* the good of putting yourself in a rage? It's a great pity; that's all one can say: it's very unfortunate: but of course it can't be helped, and it might have been ever so much worse. There's no such great harm done, after all. These Giffords are not so very much in society; the thing won't be much known or talked about. It can't be, unless you go making a foolish uproar about it, which will be in the worst possible taste, and really imprudent. It will affect your future chances in other quarters, seriously; it will damage your prestige. The match was a fairly advantageous one, all things considered, and especially if the title is to slip through your fingers; but it's not more than that. There is no real reason, as I've told you before, why a young fellow like you shouldn't do better—a great deal better. I'm sure, with a little looking about, something quite as desirable might be found for you. Not this season, of course; it's too late for that; but you lie quiet for a few months, and you'll come out again as fresh as paint in the winter. Meanwhile drop all this Edmund-Kean sort of rant about revenge. It's rubbish, I tell you. And don't quarrel with these Gifford people. Why should you? It seems a good sort of a house for dinners and that kind of thing, and the man's lent you money; there can be no possible good in making him your enemy. You can't hurt him; and he may annoy you considerably. Come, Clem, old fellow, get these notions out of your head," the Colonel said kindly, tapping him on the shoulder. "Take a turn with me in the park, and then we'll dine together. We'll have some of the best Burgundy the Club can give us, or I don't mind a run down to Greenwich to eat whitebait, if you like, though the fish are getting rather large. You'll be quite a new creature afterwards."

But Clem only shook his shoulder away from his uncle's playful tapping, and went on grinding his teeth, biting his nails, very angry indeed; still muttering menaces, and vowing to be avenged. And he didn't caress his light moustache now; he fairly tugged at its delicate points in a way that threatened to destroy them altogether.

The Colonel watched him for a few minutes with patient sadness. He was old and battered, ungodly and graceless, hard and heathen, and very selfish; yet in his padded, corrupt old bosom there existed some stray atoms of tenderness and regard for his brother's son. He avowed to himself that he liked the boy; that he was handsome and clever above others of his age and standing; a dunce at books, very likely, but still one to make his way in the world, to succeed with men and women, the latter especially, and secure of attaining a position of some advantage at last. He couldn't, he owned, see the lad so bent on going a mucker—so he phrased it—without an attempt at setting him right—without stretching out a helping hand. He didn't understand Clem's state of mind; couldn't see anything in a love disappointment to justify the wrath that led to the doing of foolish things; he thought the young fellow was talking and acting absurdly. Still he pitied him; was sorry for him; was anxious, if he could, to set him right.

"I fear I bore you, Clem," he said.

Clem did not contradict him. The Colonel began to march up and down heavily, with a sombre expression on his fleshy, red, wrinkled face. When he spoke again, there was a curious unevenness in his voice, which still possessed its cathedral-organ sort of tone; but with the addition, as it now seemed, that the *tremolo* stop was being made use of, imparting a pathetic character to the music of his speech.

"Look here, Clem," he said slowly; "I am an old fellow, you know. I can't expect to be knocking about many years more; and I don't feel that I am anything like the man I was. I feel I've changed a good deal for the worse of late. One can never quite get over the effects of that infernal climate; and I met Pottleby quite by chance the other day; and he warned me that I ought to take deuced good care of myself,—he was our doctor in India, you remember, Clem,—he knows my constitution well, and he's not a man who goes in for frightening fellows about their health unnecessarily; but he talked about fatty degeneration—that kind of thing—in a way I didn't fancy, I own. Now we've always been very good friends, you know, Clem, you and I have. There's been no humbug between us. I've never set up for a moraliser;

I've never gone in for preaching and teaching, or anything of that sort; though you *are* my nephew, I've never interfered with you; I've always held that young fellows should have their fling, without any meddling from us old boys; and so I've always treated you from a friendly point of view, as though you were some one else's son, and not poor George's. Now I do wish you'd humour me in this matter, Clem; it isn't very much I ask; but I shouldn't like to—to slip off the hooks, in fact, with anything like ill blood between us. Give in, Clem. Get away from these Gifford people for a time. Abandon the whole concern. Indeed, it isn't worth another thought. And look here: I'm going out of town almost immediately, as I said before; Pottleby recommends Baden. Now you come with me, there's a dear boy; it shan't cost you a sou; and we'll have some fun before we come back. I'm not so old or so ill but what there's a laugh or two left in me; and, by Gad, I'm not a rich man, as you know—quite the other way, in fact; but still I'll find some money for the tables,—not much, but enough to make very fair play with; and who knows but we may break the bank between us? I've known men do it, beginning almost without a rap. Come, my dear boy, is it a bargain? Say you'll give up these infernal Gifford people, and come with me? Do; there's a dear lad."

The Colonel stopped, something flurried by his own words, his voice wheezing noisily. He passed a tawny bandanna across his forehead, and with considerable excitement glittering in his bloodshot eyes he waited for his nephew's answer. His hands quite trembled: indeed, he was experiencing quite a host of new sensations; he had never before, within his memory, been convicted of so enormous a stride from the *terra firma* of worldly wisdom into the slippery regions of sentiment, as he had been moved to take within the last five minutes. He had never been so unselfish in his life before; and he waited breathlessly, while his nephew calmly considered his proposal.

"You're very kind," Clem said coldly. "I'm much obliged to you for your offer. But I think I know my own affairs best. I shall stay and see about this business."

The Colonel turned pale; his brow clouded. That his endeavour to do a kind thing to his kinsman should be thus received! he was made ridiculous; fellows at the Club would laugh at him, if they should ever come to hear of it. To be refused, a man of his age, his standing, his bulk and presence—the boy's own uncle too, the brother of poor George, late Baron Beauflower! With trembling hands he thrust on his shining hat, and grasped his Malacca cane, and moved hurriedly to the door—he was very angry.

"I shall stay and see the thing to an end," Clem said stolidly.

"Stay, then, and be d—d to you!" cried his uncle, in quavering tones. "Go to the devil your own way, you fool, you!"

And he strode from the room, banging the door after him violently. He was scarlet in the face as he walked down Piccadilly, brandishing his cane, and looking as though he longed to challenge some one to mortal combat. But there was about him an appearance as of determination of blood to the head that was really alarming.

"Poor old Alf!" Clement laughed, as his uncle retreated; a dry, ugly, unmusical laugh.

"Do you expect to see Clement this afternoon, Clare?" Mrs. Gifford, reclining as usual on her couch in the drawing-room, inquired of her daughter.

"No, mamma, dear; that is—I don't know—but I don't think we shall see so much of Clement Buckhurst in the future," Clare softly said.

Mrs. Gifford raised the screen from her eyes, the better to look into Clare's face.

"You mean, you have rejected him, Clare?" she asked.

"Yes, mamma dear."

"You don't love him?"

"No, mamma dear."

Mrs. Gifford sighed wearily.

"He was very handsome and clever, and I'm sure very kind and good-natured," she said, in a low tone.

"It couldn't be, mamma dear; indeed, indeed, it couldn't be. Don't speak of it again," Clare cried.

"I'm very sorry, Clare. But of course your happiness is the first thing to be considered. He will probably be the next Lord Beauflower; at least so people say. And I think he was very fond of you, Clare. I never could get Mr. Gifford to say what he thought of the affair. You are sure you have rightly judged your own heart, Clare?"

"Quite sure, mamma dear."

"Tell me, Clare," Mrs. Gifford said again,

after a little while, "is it because there is any one else?"

"Don't ask me, mamma dear; don't ask me," Clare murmured, and she burst into tears, hiding her face in her mother's dress.

With her white wasted hands Mrs. Gifford caressed her daughter's golden head. She was at some loss to understand the meaning of all this hysterical sobbing.

Meanwhile Clement Buckhurst had taken a cab to journey eastward, and find out Mr. Gifford's office.

"One has no chance of talking to him in Cumberland Crescent upon such a subject. I shall find him alone in the City, probably, and can say all I want to."

He found Mr. Gifford alone, busy at his desk, with books, letters, and papers, looking rather pale and anxious. The young man was kindly received; yet with an air of surprise and amusement. There is a fashion with City men to regard rather jocosely the presence among them of an unexpected visitor from the western regions of London; to contemplate him with a sort of curious wonder, as a tropical bird might be considered, if discovered among them, by the denizens of Spitzbergen; even Mr. Gifford cracked a few jests upon the subject of Clem Buckhurst's visit to the City. But he ceased to jest when the purpose of Clem's call upon him was revealed. His manner changed altogether.

He avowed that he learnt of Clem's admiration of Miss Gray, his proposal for her hand, with extreme amazement, with real distress. He had not for one moment looked forward to anything of the kind happening. He could hardly even now persuade himself that it was true. He trusted that Clem had acted hastily; had overstated the real facts of the case; had been deceived in the state of his own feelings upon the subject. For it was necessary for him (Mr. Gifford) to affirm at once, most distinctly, that the thing could not be—was quite impossible. He had always been glad to receive Clem at his house; they had all been glad to see him, as often as he chose to come, as a friend, a valued friend, a schoolfellow of his boy Herbert, a relation in some sort of Mrs. Gifford's; but he had never dreamt of anything beyond that. It could not be, he repeated. Upon any other subject he should be happy to listen to him, but not upon this. He trusted he might not be forced to discuss the matter further. But he must be forgiven for reminding Clem that his (Clem's) position was tolerably well ascertained; and that he could be considered, by no reasonable person, as an eligible match for Clare. Clare would have money; not so much, perhaps, as people were fond of asserting; but still a considerable sum. In the situation occupied by Mr. Gifford, in regard to the lady, he was bound to protect her interests, to restrain her from contracting an imprudent engagement. He was very loth to inflict pain upon Clem; for whom, in common with the other members of his family, he had a real regard. But Clem must see himself, upon a little consideration, the justice of his (Mr. Gifford's) view.

Clem didn't see it. He was obstinate, "infernally obstinate, like all the Buckhurst's," as the Honourable Alfred had declared. He continued to urge the extent of his love for Clare, disputed the fact that his position was a disadvantageous one. Mr. Gifford inquired if he had addressed Clare herself upon the subject. Clem had to admit that he had done so; and he could not conceal that his suit had not been favourably received. Mr. Gifford laughed, not pleasantly. He asked if Clem did not regard his situation as one rather hopeless and forlorn. It was clear that he was rejected by the lady, and discouraged by her friends. Wasn't it futile, he asked, to proceed further? Wasn't it unreasonable to dream of so doing? As to his pecuniary position, Mr. Gifford suggested that he had himself grounds for being acquainted with it. He went on to hint that he was himself a creditor of Clem's, in the possession of certain acceptances which he would gladly see honoured. It was clear that Mr. Gifford was absolutely master of the situation. Finally, he stated that he had already arrived at certain conclusions relative to the disposal of Clare's hand. He did not particularize his conclusions; only it was clear that Clem had no share in them.

Clem grew very angry, as men often will do when they find themselves getting the worst of a discussion. It was not only that he was repulsed; but the war was carried into his own camp. In a most polite and gentlemanly fashion Mr. Gifford had informed him that he was no fit match for Clare Gray; and, moreover, that he was her stepfather's debtor; in the gentlest way he had even been dunned for tho money owing. It was evident that the conversation had lasted quite long enough; for Clem had begun a little to forget himself. He was raising the tone of his voice, and his face was crimson. Mr. Gifford's calmness grew icy and ironical. It was quite as well that they were interrupted; the card of another visitor was brought in, and laid before Mr. Gifford. Clem abruptly departed; in his haste he nearly knocked down a small elderly gentleman, waiting quietly in the outer office to see the head of the firm of Fordyce and Fordyce. Clem simply swore at the elderly gentleman for being in the way, flung himself into his cab, and was carried back to the West End.

He was furious: he had a violent difference with the cabman concerning his fare; he spoke vehemently to the lethargic head-porter in the hall of the Alcibiades Club; snapped at the page until that young functionary fairly shivered behind his many ranks of sugar-loaf buttons, although accustomed to sharp talk from the irascible members who are to be found in all clubs; and scared the footmen and waiters. His hand was against every man. He swore he would have signal vengeance for the shameful way in which he had been treated. He grew thirsty with the repeated utterance of maledictions, and refreshed himself with hock and Seltzer. When his hand grew steadier, he wrote a note, a very cordial and kindly note, to his friend Herbert Gifford, requesting the pleasure of his company at dinner. At first sight, perhaps, it seems a strange way of beginning his revenge upon Mr. Gifford, that he should pressingly invite that gentleman's son to dinner. But probably Clem knew what he was about: he despatched his note; and then with more hock and Seltzer, and a cigar, he felt better.

The small elderly gentleman's card was curiously studied by Mr. Gifford. The name, in large, old-fashioned letters, was "JOHN MOYLE."

"I must see him, of course. Show Mr. Moyle in."

And presently the sculptor stood in the presence of Mr. Gifford. Their meeting was rather stiff and ceremonious.

"Pray be seated. I think I can guess the object of this visit," Mr. Gifford said, with a cold smile.

"Hardly, I fancy."

"You have learnt that your brother has left—I may even say, has been dismissed my service?"

"Yes; I am acquainted with that circumstance."

"And you come to intercede for him, to beg me to take him back; but I regret very much to say——"

"Pardon, I come with no such object. You and my brother have parted company; so be it. I am not surprised; I am not sorry. It may be I should have preferred your separation years and years ago."

For a moment there was a pause; the two men sat looking fixedly at each other. Mr. Gifford was the first to speak.

"May I ask, then," he said, with some harshness of manner, "to what I am indebted for the honour of this visit?"

"I come to speak to you upon a simple matter of business. You can spare me five minutes to discuss it?"

"Certainly. Ten minutes, if you please; only you will recollect that my time is valuable."

"Everybody's time is valuable. I will be as brief as possible." The old man settled himself comfortably in his chair; and then, with cruel abruptness, began, "Miss Gray is your step-daughter, Mr. Gifford. You are in some sort her guardian, I believe. In the disposal of her hand you would probably claim to have some considerable voice and influence."

"That is so, no doubt," Mr. Gifford said, with looks of surprise. "But to what is this to lead? I really cannot see——"

"Pardon me. I am here to submit to you a proposal for the hand of Miss Gray."

"*You* are! Is this a jest? If so, it is a very bad one. On behalf of whom do you make this proposal?"

"On behalf of a young gentleman named 'Noel Tredgold.'"

Mr. Gifford started back angrily.

"This is gross impertinence," he said.

John Moyle did not appear to hear. He took snuff quietly as he proceeded.

"He is the son of Bryan Tredgold, who was known to you intimately a long time since; who was abroad many years, and died recently in Wales."

"Are you mad, that you speak to me upon this subject?" Mr. Gifford cried.

"Noel is a young man of great promise," John Moyle went on, quietly. "He is a pupil of mine. I take a great interest in his welfare—in his happiness. He has lately met Miss Gray. A friendship has sprung up between these young people, which is gradually, I take upon myself to say, ripening into love."

"This is not true," Mr. Gifford interrupted warmly. "They have never met since they were mere children. They know nothing of each other.

How dare you come to me with such a fable as this?"

"Pray be calm, sir, and be sure that I am only speaking the truth;" and in a few words the sculptor related the circumstances under which Clare had visited the studio—had encountered Noel. Mr. Gifford listened impatiently enough.

"It was very wrong; it was most improper."

The sculptor did not pay heed to these comments. He spoke of the bust of Clare.

"The work is a very charming one," he said. "I have had so small a share in it, it has been so much the work of my pupil, that I feel myself entitled to praise it highly. It would do honour to any studio. You will be proud to possess it. I think it is as pretty a bust as I have seen."

"I cannot listen to such stuff as this," Mr. Gifford interrupted rudely.

"Very good. We will keep strictly to the object of my visit—to my proposal on behalf of my young friend for the hand of Miss Clare Gray."

"Is this young man, this Noel Tredgold, as you call him, aware of your coming here upon this extraordinary mission?"

"No," John Moyle admitted. "I am bound to say that I am acting without his knowledge."

"You must be satisfied, Mr. Moyle, that the whole thing is extravagant, proposterous—cannot be entertained for a moment."

"I don't see it in that light. May I inquire what is your objection to the suit of my young friend?"

"The matter is really not worth discussion. It must be quite clear to you that the person you speak of can in no sort of way claim to be the equal of the lady in question."

"You mean not her equal in point of wealth?"

"Well, it will probably suffice to place my objection upon that ground. The young man is penniless, I presume."

"Penniless," John Moyle repeated.

Mr. Gifford laughed scornfully, and pushed his chair back, as though the discussion had been brought to a close. But the old man gave no sign of any intention to depart.

"Mr. Gifford, you owe something to these Tredgolds," he said, deliberately.

"I deny it," Mr. Gifford answered, in some confusion.

"Look back at the past, and think again whether you do not owe something to these Tredgolds."

"There is little good ever to be got in any case by raking up the past. There is none to be got here. I know to what you refer. At a proper time, to the proper parties—I deny your right to interfere at all,—I am prepared to explain and defend, if need be, my conduct in the past, in reference to—to the matter you speak of."

"Don't be angry, Mr. Gifford. Pray let us speak calmly on this subject. Say, then, you owe them nothing. Do they owe you nothing?"

"What do you mean?"

"Do they not owe you a debt of vengeance—due many years—and surely to be paid at last?" His words seemed to gather force and significance from the calmness with which he spoke. Mr. Gifford was silent; but it could be seen that he was curiously agitated.

"But I did not come here to talk in this way," John Moyle resumed presently, in a gentler tone. "I want to make peace, not war. I do not wish to rake up the past, as you call it; but if possible, to bury it more securely than ever. Noel Tredgold loves Clare Gray. Give her to him. Make the young man a friend; and if he should ever know, he will soon forget, that he has had deep cause to be your enemy."

"His friendship and his enmity are alike nothing to me. It is quite clear that he can be no fit match for Miss Gray; if, indeed, I had not already arrived at other conclusions in regard to the disposal of her hand."

"You mean that she is pledged to another?"

"Not exactly. An offer has been made in regard to her—quite recently—which I have taken upon myself to decline." (The old man brightened as he heard this.) "But it is due to her that I should entertain no proposal from a quarter manifestly unworthy of her. Now, pray let us speak no more on this subject."

"One moment." John Moyle now betrayed more excitement—drew a long breath, passed his handkerchief across his forehead, nerved himself as for an effort. "You treat Noel Tredgold as her inferior, because she is an heiress——"

"She is so to some extent," Mr. Gifford interrupted.

"And he is, as you say, penniless. How if that difficulty can be got over?"

"Pardon me. I fail to understand you."

"Simply, I am a richer man than I was twenty years ago, Mr. Gifford; and I've been a cautious man—saving—miserly, some have gone so far as to say. Still, I can spend money freely upon occasions. I will do so now. Noel is to me as an adopted son. *I* owe something to these Tredgolds;" he lowered his voice to a whisper; "and I would gladly do something by way of payment of that debt. Listen; I will equalize the positions of Clare Gray and Noel Tredgold. For every pound of her fortune, I will pay down on the nail in hard cash an equal pound on behalf of Bryan Tredgold's son. Pound for pound, their fortunes shall weigh the same. Will that do?"

He spoke at last with a sort of gasp. With trembling hands, not knowing what he did, he was winding his handkerchief round and round tightly, as a laundress wrings out linen. He was quite conscious of the prodigality of the offer he had made. He was fairly amazed, frightened at it. Yet he had no thought of withdrawing from his proposal. He had not determined upon it without due deliberation; it cost him some painful effort to make; but being made, there it was; he wouldn't go back from it one hair's breadth.

"Will that do?" he asked hoarsely.

"Your offer is a very generous one, Mr. Moyle," was the answer. "There is something almost Quixotic about it. Yet I respect, though

I fail to comprehend absolutely, an act of disinterestedness so remarkable. This young man has cause to be deeply grateful to you. But——"

"You mean it won't do?" John Moyle asked, with spasmodic eagerness.

"Under no circumstance could I sanction such a union as you propose. In plain words, you will be good enough to understand that Clare Gray cannot marry the son of Bryan Tredgold; in other words, *the son of a convicted felon!* Now, if you please, we will drop the subject."

Mr. Gifford spoke with a stern frankness of manner, that had something cruel and defiant about it.

"Ah! you shift your ground. It is not the money merely."

"You are right. It is not a question of money merely."

"And *you* can speak of Bryan Tredgold in that way!" John Moyle seemed rather to address the words to himself than to Mr. Gifford. He was depressed, abstracted. His strangely generous offer was declined—simply put on one side; the sacrifice he had nerved himself to make was not necessary. Yet there was no comfort to him, as it seemed, in the thought that his money was his own again—securely his—not to be lavished in the wild, profuse way he had proposed. He remained motionless, silent for some time; when he spoke again it was in a lowered, subdued tone, with a calm, sad air.

"Be it so, Mr. Gifford," he said. "A wilful man will have his way. I interfered only because I hoped to do good. I interfere no more. Things must take their course, since you will have it so; the consequences will rest with you."

"I am prepared to accept them. You may do your worst, Mr. Moyle."

"No, no. Don't speak to me like that, sir. I hold out no threat. I have no wish or thought to do you an injury. I only ask to go on my own way. I stepped from it for a moment only in the hope that some reparation might be made for what I hold to be much wrong done in the past—wrong in which I had some share. The arrangement I looked to make shall not, cannot be, you tell me. If it ever should be, therefore, it will be in spite of you; it will be also without aid from me. I go now." Slowly he put on his hat, still lingering as though he wanted to say something more.

"Good morning, Mr. Moyle," Mr. Gifford said stiffly.

"You are a hard man, sir. Years have not

changed you in that respect, though they have wrought changes with you in other matters. You have prospered greatly; yet you are very stern and cruel and relentless still. The issue is in Heaven's hands, after all; and Heaven is very just. As you have sown so you may reap yet. God is wiser than man, and He will choose His own time to reward and to punish. Amen."

And, without a word of leave-taking, he passed slowly and solemnly out of Mr. Gifford's room.

The books, and papers, and writings remained for a long time untouched. Mr. Gifford bent over as though absorbed in the study of them. But his eyes were without speculation for them. His thoughts were far otherwise occupied. He leant his head upon his thin, tremulous hands. He looked very old, and thin, and white. When he changed his position, it was to press his hands upon his heart, as though to keep down some pain within that was very restless and acute, troubled him greatly, was preying upon his life, and would not be still.

"A strange old man," he muttered. "I never knew him really until now. I have not done him justice, perhaps. What wild, romantic folly makes him take up with this wretched boy?

'Prospered greatly,' he said; and it sounds like truth." He sneered mockingly at this. "But prospered to what end?" He pondered a long time over the train of thought this question seemed to lead to.

"It was a good offer,—a wildly generous offer. But it mustn't be. Clare shall not be handed over to this paltry workman. As I have begun, so I must go on to the end. And she cannot care for him. He can be nothing to her; he shall be nothing. I will take all necessary precautions. They shall not meet again. And her marriage shall be hurried on. It has become important that there should be no more delay; I must stir myself, and begin to work again."

And the necessity for action roused him from the curious, dreamy, listless state into which he had fallen.

He remained until a late hour at his office, toiling hard.

CHAPTER III.

"THE LITTLE GRAY GIRL."

THE words were spoken at last: "I love you, Clare."

Of course he had vowed to himself that he would never make this confession; that he would lock the secret of his passion closely in his inmost heart, and die rather than reveal it. H would not, by speaking, dissolve an illusion tha was so delicious; would not rashly sacrifice the rich certainty of her regard and friendship for the poor chance—for so it seemed to him—of her love. He would go on wrestling with his passion—mastering it in time; and she should never know.

This was the conduct he planned for himself, after wearisome days and wakeful nights of doubt and dread, much self-torture and cruel anxiety. Grand resolutions—if he could but have kept to them. Poor Noel!

He buried his secret securely, as he thought;

but it was mere snow he was heaping over and stamping down upon it, and it needed but the summer sunshine of her eyes to drill through the fragile, fleeting covering, and let air, and light, and exposure in upon his mystery. He hid his love in a fireproof safe, with many locks, and bolts, and clamps, and clasps; yet a secret spring lightly touched by the tip of a taper finger, and all these gave way, and his secret was out, free, at large.

The thing came about very simply. The bust was completed; the sculptor and the sitter were to part—to meet again, how or when, neither knew nor could guess. Indeed, they were both too troubled with the present to burden themselves with the superadded difficulty of thought of the future. For the present had its distresses; each felt how hard, how very hard, it was to part from the other, when the period of their next meeting was left so painfully vague and uncertain. And Clare put forth her hand to say, "Good-bye." She had tried to say the word some ten times before, had hitherto failed altogether, pretermitting the ceremony of leave-taking. She uttered the sad word at last, however; but so plaintively and softly, that it seemed to make parting more than ever impossible; or at least to defer it some time longer. And when Noel's fingers closed upon her hand—which they did with the tightest, tenderest sort of grip—it occurred to him somehow that he couldn't, though he tried ever so, relax his hold—couldn't let loose again that dear, soft, warm, white little prisoner upon any terms. As she couldn't, of course, go away leaving her hand behind her, she waited, with timid, blushing patience, until it should seem good to him to let her go. But he couldn't; and so they stood still, close together, until—until the great love restless in his heart suddenly broke all bonds, leaped up to his lips, took the shape of the best words he could find, —they were quite intelligible and significant enough for the purpose,—and Clare knew all.

Of course she knew it beforehand—she must have known it; but knowing it from herself was nothing to knowing it from him. If she had heard the words from a thousand lips, it would have recked nothing, if she had not heard them from his. But now he had spoken, it was true, certain, beyond all doubt or question—for had not *he* said so? He loved her!

What magic there was in the words! Foolish Noel had feared to utter them, lest they should break up utterly a lovely dream. Why, they made it a reality; they gave it life, and substance, and endurance, beyond all change, or chance of change; they invested a cloudy shadow with vitality, and form, and secure outline. Their love was a positive thing now, to be comprehended and grasped; no longer a mere floating fancy, unowned, uncertain in value, shapeless, inchoate, incoherent. And the barriers that had separated them, and which these words struck down to the earth as with a blow! Their hearts rushed together now unhindered, unprisoned. The conventionalites in which people disguise their thoughts and wrap up their words, the artificialness with which the world is wont to coat nature and conceal feeling, the thousand and one small restraints upon demonstration were flung away to the winds.

The colour left her cheeks for a moment, to return suddenly in a crimson rush; her heart throbbed turbulently; her bosom rose and fell in grand undulations of emotion; the tears clung thickly to her eyelashes. Then, with a gentle, swooning sort of tenderness, the golden head was nestling upon his breast.

"Dear Noel! you love me?" she murmured ever so softly.

She couldn't hear him too often assure her of the fact. He strained her to his heart, and kissed her. The action gave delightful accent and meaning to the words.

"Dear Noel!" and then she fondled his hand in hers; the golden head resting next his heart, as though in its proper place and quite at home there, and parting now to be postponed indefinitely, if not voted useless altogether.

There was little said at first, and their words were chiefly repetitive.

"Dearest Clare!"

"Dearest Noel!"

"You love me?"

"You know I do."

And so on, over and over again.

By and by, as they became in some measure accustomed to and assured of the idea of their love, they enlarged upon it,—seldom straying far from the original theme, however; keeping that always in view, just as a skilful pianist midst a cloud of embroideries and ornamentations always keeps well in hand the notes of the air upon which he has founded his fantasia. But what exquisite pleasure to them both to investigate this new feeling—new in its discovery, not in its existence,—which held them in so strong a union now,—strong as fetters of massy gold,—though yesterday it had seemed a mere withe in its strength to bind! To trace back their love, long ago, to its source; noting the small events that were as so many landmarks in its course! This word, that action, this look, that blush, all seeming so little at the time; and yet now, read by the bright light of their confessed affection, so full of meaning, so precious in value! And then to marvel that the avowel of their love had been so long delayed, when at every moment it seemed on the point of breaking out of itself into the light; when, with all their watchfulness, betrayal was so imminent, so constantly close to them. Noel was himself amazed he had so long hesitated to speak, when he considered the pain it had cost him to be silent; yet how could he be sure, he asked, that Clare would not be angry with him—would not reject his suit, and scorn his love?

Clare only answered in a soft musical laugh, that had nothing like rejection in it, or anything so severe, or, indeed, anything—but love.

"I did not dare, Clare dearest; I did not dare!"

"You silly Noel!"

And she kissed him.

There was more talk of the same kind; perhaps the reader has had quite enough of it set forth. The converse of lovers is proverbially uninteresting to bystanders. It was very nice, and fond, and tender to them; but likely enough it would have seemed very foolish to everybody else.

And Noel spoke of Bryan Tredgold, his father, dead in Llanderych churchyard; while Clare listened with hushed, solemn, watchful pity. Then, with a spasm of alarm,—dreading its effect upon her and her love,—he told the story Bryan had revealed upon his deathbed; of the poor soul's trials, and sufferings, and cruel doom; of his being torn from his country, a convict, his terrible life in the penal settlement, and his return home, to end his days so pitifully, a ganger upon the Welsh railway. Noel asked her, would this make her repent her love? would she think him unworthy of her? could she bear this disgrace?

She had but one answer to many questions of this kind; and her answer was in some sort interrogative. She drew the nearer to him, and whispered more tenderly than ever, if that was possible.

"Dear Noel, you love me?"

"Bryan, my poor father, was innocent, Clare."

She was certain of it.

But I don't believe that, if he had been guilty, it would have made any difference to her. She loved Bryan through Noel; but then Noel was a very engrossing subject: he hardly left any surplus of love for any one else.

Of course they had to part at last: all things come to an end. So did this interview of the lovers—after a duration of some hours though.

"We shall meet again very, very soon," she said, resuming her diaphanous bonnet. "What a shameful time I've kept the carriage waiting! Your fault, sir! Very, very soon. Don't look so sad!"

He vowed, for the thousandth time, that he couldn't bear to let her go.

"But I must, dearest; indeed I must." The daintiest of gloves were being slid on to her tiny hands.

She would come again—to-morrow, if possible. What could hinder her? Nothing. She loved him. Did he want to be told so again? Yes, he did; over and over again. She would be in the Park in the afternoon; at the Opera in the evening—the box was on the pit-tier; at Madame Some-one's morning concert on the morrow. Should she see him at any or all of these places? If he knew how happy it would make her to see him, if it was but for a minute —the merest glimpse of him! And next time they would talk more of the future: to-day they had been so occupied with the present and the past. Once more, good-bye; and then once again. A whispered question repeated; a last kiss, positively the last; and she was gone.

The studio was very dark and desolate without her; but for a time his great elation prevented his fully appreciating this fact. She had left behind her so much for his mind to dwell upon, he was so intoxicated with his great love of her, that he could not for some time come down to being reasonable and calmly reflective. He could not for a long time think anything about the different worlds in which they lived. How cruelly plain to him this had been before! He had even spoken to her upon the subject; their wide-apart social positions, and so on. It seemed now all rightly and comfortably settled somehow. She had come down from her world to him in his; as a star might descend from heaven to give itself to a mortal. Who could object, if she did not? She loved him; and he loved her with his whole soul. They were all in all to one another. What mattered anything or anybody else? For a time he could not think of his own forlorn, orphaned, dependent situation; did not remember that she was an heiress, and he—something like a pauper; had no thought for Mrs. Gifford, or Mr. Gifford, or Herbert, or Clem Buckhurst, except for a moment to marvel at his own idiocy in being jealous; did not see the utter absurdity of a convict's son—Bryan Tredgold's boy—aspiring to the hand of the daughter of the Honourable Ferdinand Gray, of the rich branch of the Grays, formerly attached to the Embassy at Naples; or question what the world would say; or shrink back at the numberless obstacles society would interpose to prevent a union that would on all hands be voted as shameful, and ridiculous, and monstrously absurd.

He started at hearing a low chuckling laugh behind. He turned, to find leaning against the door Barty Trinder, wiping his mouth with the back of his hand, oftentimes flattening his nose by proceeding unsteadily with that occupation; leering and winking with cunning, rather tipsy eyes.

"I come in once before, but I went out again, because I found you—*busy*." He chuckled greatly here. "I went out to drink somebody's 'ealth." He laid his finger on his nose with an artful expression. It may be said that he did not refer to himself: his drinking had been entirely without reference to his own health; he was, indeed, far from sober. "I think I should like to drink somebody's health again."

"Here you are, then, Barty."

Noel laughed, and flung him a sovereign.

It was very foolish; but the young man was in a state of some excitement; he was in great good humour with the whole world; he would have taken the very clothes from his back, and given them to the first comer, upon the slightest hint of his needing them,—he was so exalted by his love. It was madness to give Barty the means of further drinking. If Mrs. Trinder had known! But she never did. You see, it's difficult in the case of a drunken man to assess exactly the amount it has cost him to become a beast; I mean the amount to be understood in a monetary, not a moral sense. The thing can be done at such a variety of prices,—at a great expense, or upon very moderate terms,—according as the drinker affects wines of cost or spirits of cheapness. Whatever else Barty consumed, he had very little change left out of the sovereign at nightfall. He was then in a dreadful state. His wife, with prompt decision, put him under the pump in the back kitchen for half-an-hour, and plied the handle vigorously. But cold water on the outside is but a poor way, after all, of getting under the fire raging within. As well try to put out the flames gutting a house by pumping on the external walls.

"She loves me!" cried Noel, as the sculptor entered.

The young man couldn't keep the knowledge of that fact to himself. He thought, fatuously, that by sharing the knowledge with his friends he distributed amongst them also the joy it afforded to him. But lovers are so unreasonable, so selfish. Do your best to show sympathy with, to express congratulation upon, their exhilaration, and yet they think you always cold and niggardly, and perhaps jealous and doubting. You can't climb to their pitch of excitement—it's simply impossible; and so they vote your inability flat treason, and denounce you as unfeeling and ungenerous.

"She loves me!" cried Noel a second time, in louder, clearer tones, lest he should have been misunderstood; and then he looked as though he expected his preceptor to stand on his head and clap his heels together out of pure delight, or to proceed to blow up his studio with gunpowder by way of reckless *feu de joie*, or do some other deed, no matter how mad, by way of exhibiting satisfaction at the glorious news.

"Tell me something I don't know," John Moyle growled, and turned away.

Perhaps he might have said more than that; and Noel had some right to be disappointed.

Mrs. Trinder somehow managed to hear of the affair, and was more demonstrative, after the manner of her sex on such occasions.

"Well, Mr. Noel, I give you joy. She's a pooty creetur, let who will say she isn't." She looked at him rather sternly, as though he had been hinting some such thing: which of course he hadn't. "I see her get into her carriage; and her boots were lovely, and the lace round her handkercher couldn't have been less than a guinea a yard. As for her bonnet——"

And it seemed that, upon the whole, Mrs. Trinder laid more stress upon the lady's dress than anything else.

"She'll make you a darling of a wife, Mr. Noel. I'm sure the silk of her skirt would have stood up of itself." As if he had been going to marry a silken skirt, however superior!

Of course he went wherever there was the smallest chance of meeting Clare—to the Park, to the Opera, everywhere; valuing a soft glance from her eyes, a sweet smile dancing upon her lips, the mere sight of her when she was looking another way even, as worth every other thing in Hyde Park, as beyond all the music-composer had ever composed, or the best of Opera-singers had ever sung, or the most aristocratic audiences had ever listened to, or not listened to, talking instead.

He even lingered at midnight near the iron railings round the gardens of Cumberland Crescent, of course hopeless of seeing her, but satisfied with the thought that he was not far from her, that he was nearer to her than he would be in Quebec Street. He tore himself away reluctantly at last; only to go home and dream of her.

His love possessed him very absolutely; as love has possessed a good many millions of young people before him, ever since the world began.

Mrs. Gifford lay shivering on her sofa, as she listened to a conversation going on in an adjoining room between her daughter and Mr. Gifford. She trembled for Clare, and for herself; for Mr. Gifford, it was evident, was very angry.

"Clare, you did wrong to go to Mr. Moyle's," he said, sternly.

Clare did not answer. She knew that this was unjust, when the intention and object of her going to the sculptor's were duly considered.

"I hate secrecy," he went on; "it is too nearly allied to treachery and deceit. I never thought to have to lay such things to your charge, Clare."

She was pained at this; winced visibly under his words; but she did not speak.

"You have made acquaintances you never ought to have made. You have met people you never should have met with my sanction. This crazy old sculptor, the accomplice of a worthless designing adventurer, named, it seems, Noel Tredgold——"

"Not a word against him!" she said suddenly, with a passion that startled Mr. Gifford. "I cannot, I will not listen to a word against Noel Tredgold!"

"What can this man be to you, Clare?"

"I love him," she said, with simple fervour.

Mr. Gifford bit his lip.

"My poor Clare," he resumed presently, "there has been a conspiracy against you. You are not fit to deal with these matters. There has been a snare spread for you, and you are caught in it. Do you know who this man Tredgold is?

Doubtless he has been very careful to hide from you the real truth. He is without a penny in the world; has worked as a common labourer; is the son of a convicted felon——"

"I know it," she interrupted; "I have learned this from his own lips. He has kept back nothing from me."

"But he has spun a fine coating of romance for his story, doubtless. He told you his father was innocent?"

"Yes! And I believed him; I believe him still." Mr. Gifford gave a low, mocking laugh. Clare's face crimsoned. "But innocent or guilty," she said, warmly, "it matters not; it does not affect me. I love him."

Mr. Gifford paused. He was taken by surprise. He had not been prepared for a resistance so determined, for Clare's taking up with opinions so decided, for her valiant assertion of them. Perhaps he had a little misunderstood her; had underrated her strength of will; or had not sufficiently recognized the fact that love makes a great change in a woman, lends her occasionally a force and energy that may seem foreign to her character as it had been previously considered.

When he spoke again, it was with a prudent

change of tone. He saw that direct opposition was thrown away, or would at least simply drive the lady to adopt extreme courses; would compel a direct conflict with her. He adopted a gentler policy.

"I am deeply grieved at this, Clare," he said, quietly; "I have lately had some trouble with Herbert in a case of misdirected affection. I did not reckon to be distressed even more acutely by conduct of yours under similar circumstances. More acutely distressed, I say, because the situation of a woman in these affairs is surrounded by difficulties ten times more trying than can occur in the case of a man. I am deeply grieved. It has been my happiness to regard you both as my children, to treat you with quite equal affection, to make this a happy home for both of you. In return for my love, I did look, I own, for confidence—for at least consideration. If you could not feel towards me as a daughter feels for her father——"

His voice faltered a little, with real or well-assumed emotion.

Clare was touched. In her present state of nervous, acutely sensitive agitation, his air of kindness and tenderness of tone moved her deeply.

"I have felt this, indeed I have," she murmured; and she took his hand.

"If I have failed," he went on, "after much effort, to supply the place of that father it pleased Providence to deprive you of long years since, when you were a mere infant, I did think, Clare, I had succeeded in making you regard me as a friend—a true, fond friend. I don't remember ever treating you with harshness. I can charge myself with no lack of kindness. If I have been stern and harsh with others—and people have so said of me, I know—surely I have never been so to you?"

"No, no, indeed not," she said; and the tears stood in her eyes.

"I admit that I have had views of my own on the subject of your marriage, which I have always prayed might be a happy one, might not wholly separate you from me and mine," he proceeded, with some hesitation. "I had thought, indeed, that, not immediately, but in the course of time, you might in my son Herbert find a husband who——"

But this suggestion, so new, so unexpected, shocked her seriously, he could see. She had never, she could never, dream of a union with Herbert. She had regarded him as a brother ever, and no more. She was fairly frightened at any other idea in regard to him being presented to her. At any time she would have shrunk from it; but more than ever now. Mr. Gifford saw that it would be mischievous to proceed further with that branch of his subject; he was undoing all the good effected by the moderation and kindliness of his previous efforts.

"But at least I thought," he went on, "I hoped, that the object of your regards would be some one worthy of you." She was about to interrupt, but he checked her: "Let me say, then, some one whom I could approve; whose union with you would be with the full sanction of your mother, and every member of your family. In the present case you must be well assured, Clare, the man for whom you have expressed a most unhappy preference can never be in any way received or recognized by us, far less approved."

He waited, perhaps expecting her to say something; but she was silent, with her eyes fixed upon the ground.

"Herbert," he said, "has complied with my wishes; has abandoned his thoughtless love affair. Will you do less, Clare?"

There was some adroitness in reducing the importance of her love for Noel to a level with

Herbert's preference for Liz Moyle. She could hardly resent the comparison. Yet it threw contempt and degradation upon her love and her lover.

"Will you do less, Clare?"

"I love him," she moaned; the tears streamed down her face.

"I do not dispute your love. I know that I am asking you to do what will cause you some suffering; what must seem to you a very cruel sacrifice; what is indeed very difficult to you to do. Yet should it not be done, Clare?"

"Am I to count his feelings for nothing?"

"Are you to count our feelings for nothing, Clare?—your mother's—mine—all who know you? I tell you, Clare, the marriage you dream of would break our hearts; for it would take you from us for ever."

"But Noel?" she cried, piteously.

"He will suffer, of course. But he is a man: he will bear it as a man should."

Wisely Mr. Gifford refrained from further abuse of her lover, which he saw only strengthened her opposition. He felt indeed that he was gaining ground: he had brought her to discuss the matter, to reason upon it. So long as she was behind the shelter of her sentiments, her position was impregnable.

"Do not throw away those who have known and loved you all your life for the sake of one with whom your acquaintance must be very, very recent. For it amounts to that, Clare. Your choice is between us and him. Have we no claim upon your affections? Do you dream for a moment, my poor child, that our love for you can be less whole and true than his? Clare, do not abandon us; do not break our hearts."

"What am I to do?" she cried. And she covered her face with her hands.

"Be true to yourself, Clare, and remember what is due to your family and your position. God bless you, my dear Clare! I will say no more now. You will think over what I have said. I leave all to your own sense of duty. To do what is right, no matter the cost, is to deprive a sacrifice of half its suffering."

And he left her.

"What am I to do?" Clare asked again, in a broken voice, as she sobbed upon her mother's bosom.

"O Clare, my darling," Mrs. Gifford answered, greatly frightened, "do whatever papa tells you. Indeed it will be for the best; be sure it will."

Of course more was said upon the subject—a great deal more. She had other conversations with her stepfather. He was kind, but firm. He would not listen to the notion of her marrying Bryan Tredgold's son. Clare suffered terribly. Her eyes were for ever filling with tears, her voice breaking into sobs. She grew strangely weak and nervous, pale and trembling. But she wouldn't give up Noel.

This family contest was carried on with vigour. But a sort of armed truce was at length agreed upon.

There was to be a cessation of hostilities for a stated period, without surrender of principles. Clare's desires were not to be further combated; no new influence was to be brought against her; no other plans for her marriage entertained. Her love for Noel was to be regarded as a sealed subject. Nothing was to be said anent it one way or the other. She consented, on the other side, to forego seeing or writing to him, or forwarding her engagement with him in any way. Time—a short time, it was hoped—would settle the question altogether. These terms were favourable to Clare. Her health and strength were giving way in the protraction of the struggle. She was permitted, however, to inform her lover by letter of the agreement that had been arrived at.

Noel was in despair. He construed the letter as disastrous to his love.

"All is over!" he cried, in great anguish. "They have taken her from me. I shall never see her again. My darling Clare! I have lost her for ever!"

And he conducted himself like a madman. The lover is at no time a very reasonable creature; in his moments of despair he passes all the bounds of common sense. His despondency was not less extravagant than his elation had been. Clare lost to him! He wanted to die at once, and end the business. For what had he now to live? What was life worth to him without Clare? Nothing.

He showed the letter to John Moyle, imploring his advice, without question as to whether or not he should follow it when obtained. Perhaps he simply meant consolation; but he asked for counsel.

"Forget her," the sculptor said, abruptly.

"You have never loved," the young man cried, scowling. And he turned away in a passion.

"I have never loved?" John Moyle repeated after him, grimly. But his manner changed in a moment; he saw how much Noel was in earnest, how really he suffered. "My poor boy!" he said—and he patted him kindly on the shoulder —"indeed I feel for you. And I know how to: for I in my time have loved, and been bitterly disappointed. It seems strange now—foolish—doesn't it, to think of my loving? A poor, rough old man like me, with white hair, and a figure all out of drawing, and a rude, red face—to think of my loving! It seems madness almost. Yet it's true, Noel. Years ago I loved, with all my soul, as it seemed to me no one had ever loved before, or could love again. I suppose all lovers think that. Yes; *I* loved once. Once, do I say? God help me; I love still!"

He was strangely agitated; his voice broke into a tremulous wail. For a moment they seemed to have changed places; the young man forgetting his own great need of comfort, was seeking to calm and console the elder.

"Does it help you to think that there have been others who have suffered as you are suffering, who have been as utterly cast down and wretched? I have been so—long ago now. Yet something of my anguish survives still—is at times as fresh and cruel and intense as ever."

"Don't speak of this now," Noel cried, soothingly.

"It was hard to bear; yet I live still, you see. I can even laugh and joke and be merry now and then." He said this with such a piteous effort to smile; but he failed altogether, and sobbed instead. "You wouldn't think I have ever suffered as I have. Worse than you, my poor boy, worse by a great deal; for in your deepest pain you have some comfort. You can look back at the past, and hug tight to your heart the thought that you were loved once. That was not for me; I couldn't do that. She never cared for me, never thought of me. My love was wholly wasted; she had given her heart to another. O Noel, don't ruin your young life. Try and tear yourself away from a love without hope. It cannot be, Noel. You are struggling against one who is too powerful to be resisted; who is without mercy, without pity; who will crush you, as he has crushed others."

He spoke with passion. To Noel his words were only vaguely intelligible; especially he could not comprehend the warning contained in the latter sentences. He tried to hinder the vehemence, to calm the passion, which was agitating the old man so greatly. But the sculptor seemed to take a curious pleasure in his violence. He would not be stayed.

In a moment he had drawn Noel to the recess in the side of the room farthest from the door, and drawn the curtain which hung before it. He pointed to the marble medallion-portrait fastened to the wall.

"I told you it was a commission given me years back—never paid for, and so left here. That was not true. It is *her* portrait, Noel. Could I help loving her?"

"She was very beautiful," Noel said, as his eyes wandered over the delicate outlines of the face, the waving hair loosely gathered into a knot low down at the back of the head, and tenderly streaked with dead gold; the lightly tinted wreath of flowers; and the pink-stained lips.

"And she is dead?" he asked softly, his voice lowered by his admiration and his sympathy.

"Yes; she is dead," John Moyle answered with a gasp. He glanced with a frightened air from the portrait to Noel, then back again to the portrait. Then, in a wild, hurried tone, he cried, "Why should I hide it from you longer? My poor Noel, *it was your mother!*"

Pale and trembling, the old man snatched up his hat, and with staggering steps quitted the studio.

Noel stood—painfully agitated, his heart throbbing fiercely—facing the portrait of his mother—the mother he had never seen or known in any way, concerning whom he had oftentimes ransacked his memory for the poorest trace—how vainly! He stood gazing at the lovely face until his tears blinded him. He had seen the portrait before—contemplated it with interest even, yet never dreaming of the sure claim it had upon his reverence, his love. His mother! What a sweet, tender face, even in marble! What would he have given to have seen it living!

For some time he remained in front of the medallion. He turned with a sudden start, for he felt the presence of some one else in the studio close to his elbow. It was William Moyle, with flushed face, swollen features, and unsteady, bloodshot eyes.

"A pretty thing," he said thickly; "one of John's fancies. Nice looking woman—a great flame of John's."

Noel hardly heard him; he was gazing abstractedly at the marble.

"Dead, dead!" he said.

"No, not dead," the other cried, with sudden loudness. "Bless you, no; only it's a secret. The woman lives still. I know all about it."

"Lives?" Noel asked, with a scream of anxiety.

"Yes; of course she does. I'll tell you all about it; not now, though—some other day, because"—he lowered his voice, and half-closed his eyes with an expression of tipsy cunning—"because, you know, John would be in such a way. And he's coming back; don't you hear his footsteps? It won't do for me to offend him, because, don't you see, he's lent me money of late; it won't do to offend him. Some other day; some other day."

CHAPTER IV.

"AWAY WITH MELANCHOLY."

THE cutting off of one's nose with the view of being revenged upon one's face is not, of course, a very reasonable proceeding; but then, from an abstract point of view, revenge in itself is not perhaps, remarkably reasonable. Such at least was, as we have seen, Colonel the Honourable Alfred Buckhurst's view of it: albeit Lord Bacon has said that "revenge is a sort of wild justice;" very wild indeed, sometimes, it must be allowed. But were it never so unreasonable, it probably would not be on that account a less favourite line of conduct than it now is with a great many of our fellow-creatures, who have often a certain proneness for doing what is fatuous and futile.

Clem Buckhurst had sworn to be avenged for the rejection of his suit by Clare Gray. And one branch of his method of vengeance took a curious form. He busied himself, with a childish persistence and spitefulness, in doing many things which he knew would be decidedly disapproved by her. He did not pause to ask whether she would ever learn of his new behaviour, or whether he was not simply inconveniencing himself by its adoption. As she would have liked him to lead a good and reputable life, so he led a bad and disreputable one; as she would have wished him to be sober, so he got drunk; to use fair and temperate language, so he took to talk of a foul and intemperate character; to conduct himself like a gentleman, so he behaved like a blackguard. The members of the Alcibiades Club were not easily shocked, but many of them raised murmurs against the goings on of Mr. Clem Buckhurst. He outraged propriety in a manner that was generally voted to be "a great deal too bad." Many things he said and did could be countenanced in no sort of way. Society takes broad views—is not very particular; if you will but wear the smallest scrap of a cloak, it will deem you to be very fairly concealed. You may do many improper things, if you will do them properly, with some show of privacy—as though you were, if ever so little, ashamed of them. But Clem took pains to parade his viciousness. He seemed to publish, as far and wide as possible, his constant association upon intimate terms with men who were infamous, and women who were—anything but what they should be. I don't want to use harsh words, but "frail" is really too mild for the present occasion. And poor Clare was to be punished by seeing her former lover, for whom she had once certainly some little tenderness, exhibiting himself everywhere in shameful company, her place at his side and in his heart—he seemed to wish that it should be so believed—supplied by a woman superbly dressed in the latest French fashions, but with a brazen painted face, with blackened eyelids and brows, vermillioned lips, and amply-revealed shoulders, plastered with white. Poor Clare! it would have pained her to see this, because shame and degradation and impurity would have pained her wherever found. She would have suffered, for Clem's sake. But the wanton attempt to wound and shock her failed altogether. She never knew of Clem's pitiful proceedings; they would have been more absurd if they had been less wicked. She never knew of them. And so that trumpery bit of vengeance failed absolutely.

The Honourable Alfred had gone to Baden. Something of Clem's conduct he heard from old brother officers, irregular correspondents, prompted to write now by the notion that, "By Gad! Buckhurst ought to be told of his infernal nephew's goings-on." But the Colonel did not interfere. He knew that the time had gone by for his being of any use. Clem had shaken himself loose of the very slight ties which had ever held him to his uncle. The Honourable Alfred devoted his energies to nursing his determination of blood to the head; he drank light German wines, and gambled in moderation. He looked older and sadder than of yore, all his friends agreed amongst themselves. The gallant old East Indiaman was gradually going to pieces.

So Clem Buckhurst drowned his sorrows in the bowl, a very dirty one, draining to the dregs its contents: they were not nice, perhaps, but they were intoxicating; revenging himself upon Clare by warring against the world; cutting off his nose by way of vengeance upon his face, in short.

He saw Herbert Gifford very often now, playing the part of a very worthless Mentor to that young man's most feeble Telemachus. Herbert was glad to be away as much as he could from Cumberland Crescent. He was afraid of Clare making unpleasant discoveries with regard to his "disgraceful" love-affair. The alarm was altogether needless; the lady had matters of her own requiring all her attention; day and night she was occupied now with a heart-trouble that was not Herbert's, but was a great deal nearer to her. And he dreaded all unnecessary encounters with his father, whom he had shamefully deceived, to whom he had lied disgracefully. Upon detection, he knew his father's anger would be extreme; so he kept out of his way, in case of accidents. His fears were exaggerated in this case also. Perhaps Mr. Gifford overrated his son's sense of probity and honour; did not dream of the speed with which he would go from his word of promise. He was much engaged with the affairs of Fordyce and Fordyce; with the alarming tightness of money in the City; with a proposal that had been made recently for the hand of Clare Gray; and other business arising therefrom. For some time Mr. Gifford had not given a thought to the Liz-Moyle affair.

Herbert was, as we know, precluded from visiting in Whitfield Street: the meetings in Fitzroy Square were frequent and regular, however: still they left him much spare time, and he did not find that he could spend this more pleasantly than with his old friend and schoolfellow, Clem Buckhurst, who received him with open arms, welcoming him heartily to little careful dinners at the Alcibiades and the Trafalgar—entertainments at which the amount of bread bore rather a Falstaffian proportion to the quantity of sack consumed—to be followed by a devilled something, and "just one game of cards" in Jasmin Street before parting, and the wending his way to Cumberland Crescent of Herbert Gifford in the small hours, with aching head and stumbling gait, and the symptoms of feverish festivity full upon him. But his constitution was tolerably good; his stomach was young; these excesses did not tell very much upon him the next morning. He got back his appetite with the aid of stimulants, and doses, and mixtures, well known to the convivial, by about lunch-time, and his head had given over aching by about three o'clock in the afternoon. So, altogether, he didn't do so much amiss; and he drowned his sorrows, washing away his melancholy with champagne.

"Those seas are dangerous, greybeards swear,
Whose sea-beach is the goblet's brim;
And true it is they drown Old Care,
But what care we for him,
So we but float on wine?"

He agreed with the poet; or rather he would have agreed with him if he had happened to have known anything about him or his verse. But that wasn't the case.

Lovers are very garrulous. The sweet story of their love oozes out of them all over like molasses from the seams of a cask. And then pour wine upon the fire of their passion, and doesn't it blaze up with a noisy betraying crackle that can be heard ever so far around? Of course the story of Herbert Gifford's love for Miss Elizabeth Moyle was very soon known in all its delicate details to Clem Buckhurst. It was told in a blushing, confused, prolix sort of way; yet it was sufficiently intelligible.

"Here's her health," cries Clem; "not in wine-glasses, in tumblers. *Her health!*" And he was in a hurry to get the liquor up to his lips, to hide his strong inclination to laugh, it might be. Herbert emptied his tumbler enthusiastically; and the tears stood in his eyes afterwards, resulting from emotion, or possibly from the effervescence of the wine carrying away his breath and otherwise inconveniencing him.

"I should *so* like you to see her, Clem, to have your opinion of her."

The lover is always anxious for the opinion of his confidants; not that he ever means to act upon it when obtained; least of all if it goes against his own views.

"I would give any money to see her," Clem cries, with an admirable affectation of fervour.

"She is *so* beautiful!" And Herbert goes into maundering raptures full of involved reiterations touching the marvels of Liz's beauty. Clem holds his glass up, watching the minute bubbles rise to the surface and vanish in infinitesimal fizzes, masking the strong inclination to gape which is contorting his handsome mouth.

"Now, what would you do, Clem, if you were me? What's your candid advice?" Herbert asks; and he describes once more his situation in regard to Liz, not concealing his father's sentiments upon the subject.

"If I loved her," Clem states, deliberately, "as you say you do——"

"As I do!" Herbert interposes, objecting to anything like a supposition in regard to his passion, desirous that it should be accepted at once as a certain fact.

"As you do, then," Clem goes on, "if I loved her as you do, I should most decidedly, without hesitation, *marry her.*"

"You would? Oh, thank you, Clem, for your excellent advice."

"It would be deuced hard if a man couldn't

please himself as to his own marriage. What *may* he do, if he mayn't do that?"

Clem's oracular tone was very convincing. Herbert thanked Heaven for giving him such a true friend. And then they played *écarté*.

It was whispered in the smoking-room at the Alcibiades that Clem Buckhurst, in a quiet sort of way, was cleaning out young Gifford. They know everything, the smokers at the Alcibiades. They have private and particular information on every subject; they must maintain spies, it would seem, in every court abroad and in every back-slum at home. Politicians or pugilists, bishops or ballet-girls, duchesses or demireps, are all known, and intimately, to the smokers at the Alcibiades. Just as, in the club dining-room, fish and fowl, beef and mutton, are served up by the *chef* in all sorts of dainty and ingenious ways, so in the smoking-room there are artists of even superior skill, who prepare dishes made as it were from slices cut from their neighbours, yet so choicely seasoned, so adroitly disguised, you are hardly conscious that you are, in fact, banqueting upon human flesh; a fellow-creature's heart stuck about with scandal is a piquant *plat* to pick at; a minced reputation is appetizing food; while some nice things in the way of devilling command considerable admiration. The smokers were in haste to dish up Clem as a rook, and Herbert as a pigeon. But they were a little premature. As yet young Mr. Gifford had not suffered much from playing *écarté* with his friend.

The man who succeeds in his love is often said to be sure of meeting with reverses at play. Yet this is not invariably the case. Smiled upon by Liz Moyle, Herbert did not encounter at cards the frowns of fortune. He rose repeatedly a winner. He played badly; but then his hands were so good, he could hardly have lost even if he had tried. He might have won more, but he was absorbed in other considerations. He paid no great heed to the game. Possibly that coquette Fortune, after the manner of her sex, treated him with the greater favour because he courted her so indifferently, while she turned with cold disdain upon the persistent suit of her other more faithful wooer, Clem. Game after game did not change the run of luck. Clem got up in a rage, flinging away his cards. The best play in the world would be wasted upon such luck. And Clem was greatly in want of money; a large chorus of creditors were raising their voices, until an obstreperous *crescendo* of dunning had been arrived at. He had made certain of winning from Herbert. Yet now, in lieu of having to receive, he had to pay.

Suddenly a change occurred in Clement Buckhurst's manner of life. He took to being closely occupied every morning after breakfast. He was so desirous not to be disturbed, that he locked the door of his sitting-room. He shut himself up with several packs of cards, obtained from a stationer's close by in Piccadilly. It seemed as though he were playing *écarté* and other games by himself. He took the covers from the pack with a curious caution, not tearing them abruptly off, but steaming them before the spout of his kettle, so that the cards might be drawn out without injury to the government-stamped paper enveloping them. He then subjected the cards to a remarkable course of treatment. Upon some he made slight indentations with a penknife—scratches in various places upon back and front; some he scraped or sliced a very little smaller than their fellows; others he bent carefully into a slight curve. After this he proceeded to play several games with himself. It may be noted that, by the course he had pursued, a considerable change in the luck had been effected. He dealt himself surprisingly good hands, while the most indifferent cards in the pack fell to the share of his adversary. When he tested his fortune at simply cutting the cards, the result was really marvellous. He appeared to be able to turn up any card he chose. Satisfied at length, he packed the cards back into their envelopes. With the aid of a little gum, these were neatly secured again. You would never have dreamt that they had ever been opened, and that their contents had been subjected to a manipulation so remarkable.

In plain words, of course, Clem had "doctored" the cards. He had made himself safe against a further run of bad luck. Indeed the chances were that he would now, without much difficulty, win back again the amount of his losses to Herbert Gifford. Decidedly he was a man whose play it was advisable to back if you were bound to bet upon his game with his young friend.

At the next *écarté* evening in Jasmin Street, Herbert found himself steadily losing. Otherwise it was an agreeable evening. Clem was in capital spirits; and he had brewed a bowl of *maraschino* punch from a recipe which had been obtained from Colonel the Honourable Alfred Buckhurst, who was indebted for it, so repute went, to the favour of his Royal Highness the late Duke of York. Perhaps, if the concoction had a failing, it was in the fact that the potency of the drink was excessive. Yet it seemed such a milksop sort of proceeding to reduce it by adding more water to it, that they didn't do that. They drank of it as it was; and they drank a great deal of it—a great deal too much, indeed.

When they parted, Clem had won considerably. He was less than ever inclined to regret that he had not gone to Baden with his uncle. At the table there, it is well known the odds are in favour of the bank. In Jasmin Street decidedly the odds were with him. The two friends were to meet again very shortly; when Herbert was to have his revenge!

He went on losing. If the tide of fortune flowed towards him, it was for a few minutes only: it flowed from him for long hours together. He grew very frightened at the amount of his losses; he began to be conscious at last that he was powerless to meet his engagements, that he could not hope to obtain from any quarter the means of paying his debt. Still he played on to retrieve himself. The luck must turn, he argued; to go on was his only chance. So he doubled his stakes and backed his ill luck. It was frightful; he still lost. Clem at last declined to play any more—on that occasion, at any rate. The run of fortune was so dead against his friend, that Clem was frightened at his own success. And Herbert grew desperate; he was raving like a madman. They had sat all through the night on to the noon of the following day. They stopped at last, because Herbert could no longer hold his cards—could no longer see them. White and shivering, he staggered from the table, and fell half-fainting upon the sofa.

And how was he to pay? He took William Moyle into his confidence; excepting as to the amount of his losses; that was a secret between Clem and himself. Clem entreated him not to distress himself about the money: there was no hurry *for a day or two.* He said this so repeatedly, that it was very like dunning for the amount due. He was paid at last by several oblong slips of paper. The writing of these, and especially the signature below the writing, he examined with a strange particularity. He took them to his friend Ishmael in Spring Gardens, with whom he had a jocose conversation, and who finally handed over what he called a balance of account—a check for a handsome amount—and locked the slips of paper up in an iron safe. It was curious that about the same time William Moyle had gone into the City, taking with him similar slips of paper, concerning which he had an interview with a brisk, business-like gentleman in a very diminutive office—it was more like a cupboard than a room—in the immediate vicinity of the Bank of England.

Mr. Stap had not been altogether idle. Though forbidden to enter his uncle's house, he haunted the neighbourhood; and he had discovered that Liz met Herbert very often in Fitzroy Square. But he was far from clear as to the line of conduct it was advisable for him to adopt in consequence of this discovery.

It was late one night. Mr. Stap was waiting in Whitfield Street the return of William Moyle. He looked anxiously up and down for the coming of his uncle. It was as though he had something important to communicate to him.

At length an unsteady, ungainly figure came round the corner.

"Is that you, Uncle Bill?" Mr. Stap asked, in a low tone.

"Hullo, Jemmy!" William was apparently in a good humour; he was not sober.

"I've been wanting to see you so much—about Liz."

"What about Liz?"

"She's gone away in a cab with luggage on the top; there was some one else in the cab leaning back. I think it was young Gifford."

William Moyle laughed loudly.

"Come in, Jemmy, and have a little something to drink, if it's only half a tumbler."

And he led his nephew into the house. There he broke into a noisy and prolonged fit of laughter.

"What do you think of that, Jemmy?" he asked. And he tossed over to the young man a paper, part printing, part writing.

With a pale, frightened face, wide-opened eyes, and parted lips, Jemmy Stap read through the document. It was signed by the Registrar of Marriages, Births, and Deaths in the parish of St. Pancras, and certified the marriage of Herbert Richard Gifford, bachelor, of full age, and Elizabeth Moyle, Spinster, of full age; the witnesses being Clement Adolphus Ernest Buckhurst, gentleman, and Victoria Harriet Minns, dressmaker.

"Now fill up, Jemmy," cried William Moyle, "and drink their very good healths. I've been doing it all day long. Long life and happiness to the bride and bridegroom!"

As he spoke he swayed about, lost his balance, and fell prone upon the hearthrug.

CHAPTER V.

A CLANDESTINE MARRIAGE.

"YOUR 'if' is the only peacemaker," says Touchstone; "much virtue in 'if.'"

If Clare could but have loved Clement Buckhurst, or could but have persuaded herself that she did so; if she had never met Noel Tredgold; or if he had been true to his purpose, and never made mention of his love for her, into what new and different channels, might not the current of the events of this history have been diverted? Possessed of Clare's affection, and of course her fortune, Clem would have had no need to busy himself with vengeful schemes; would have had no occasion nor desire for Herbert's ruin; would not have urged on his imprudent marriage, nor connived at the triumph of William Moyle and the frustration of Mr. Stap's hopes. He would have been quite content; not so difficult a state of mind to arrive at, when you have got all you can possibly want. He might even have developed into a creditable member of society, and have been to Clare a very tolerable sort of husband, as husbands go. Prosperous and comfortable, he might have gone on to the end, elegant, and courtly, and graceful; good fortune would have veiled his native bad qualities so completely that they might never have been discovered at all, or, at most, would have only come to the light in front of his own fireside now and then, for a man's own household *do* manage to see a little more behind his mask than other people. But this would have been in a small way only. With his every wish gratified, a man must be something of a monster who cannot comport himself with a considerable show of respectability. Ill-fortune finds men out, however: cross them, and see if they are good-humoured still; let want pinch them, and see if they are honest; let them fancy they are wronged, and see if they endure patiently or pant for vengeance. Subjected to such an ordeal, Clem Buckhurst did not emerge from it with much credit to himself. Speaking phrenologically, he had always had a plenty of "bad bumps" on his head; and opposition and ill-luck developed these in quite a dreadful degree. In a passion of vindictiveness, he was capable of "going any lengths," as people say; and he went them, as we have seen. He had no religion, of course; he had not a particle of principle; nor was he even a subscriber to any code of conventional propriety, such as, however heathen and worldly in its character, yet keeps the men who accept its authority from any very flagrant departure from a line of conduct which the society has agreed to consider honourable.

Colonel Alfred, for instance, was not a very good man—the reader has probably quite made up his mind upon that subject—but he was better than Clem. And not simply because he held revenge to be "rubbish," but he would never have stooped to being ungentlemanly, which is the world's synonym for acting dishonourably. He had a notion, no doubt, that women were sent into the world to be the toys of male creation; did not regard them very seriously; thought that a man, especially a soldier, might trifle with, and jilt, and deceive them, and yet no great harm done either; but as for any act of deliberate unkindness, any cruel retaliation, if he should be the tricked and jilted party—any systematic vengeance—he would as soon have thought of felling them with his clenched fist. And he would play cards, certainly he would; and win if he could; and he did not object to sitting down with an inferior player. "A man must learn, sir, and pay for his lessons," he would say; "it was the rule, sir, all the world over." But for playing with cogged dice, or marked cards!—suggest such a thing to the Colonel, and you stood a certain risk of being kicked down-stairs or flung from the window—whichever might be the handiest course to adopt at the moment.

If Clare had but loved Clem Buckhurst! How vast a superstructure of probabilities turns upon that small pivot! But she didn't love him; she didn't even dream that she did, but for a few minutes; otherwise she had not been the heroine of this history.

And so Clem's vengeance took its course.

William Moyle had subsided on the hearth-rug. The shock of his fall over, he accepted his situation with a sort of tipsy philosophy. He did not attempt to rise. Perhaps the assuring thought that he could not fall further, comforted him, reconciled him to his situation. He resumed his discourse—took up his text again—and, beating upon the floor with his tumbler—emptied by his accident—he continued to wish health and happiness to the bride and bridegroom, Mr. and Mrs. Herbert Gifford. He went on until he smashed the glass, and cut his hand. This stopped, if it did not sober, him. He gazed at his bleeding fingers with boozy bewilderment, as though something quite out of the nature of things had happened—as though it was a thoroughly new idea to him that glass would break if violently handled, and flesh would bleed when lacerated. He then took to whining over the occurrence, holding up his hand in a piteous complaining way, and then trying clumsily to bind his wound up with his pocket-handkerchief. This was more than he could manage, however; and he relinquished the attempt in an effort to find a drop or two of liquor still left in the fragment of his tumbler—the salvage of the accident.

"Help me up!" he cried.

But Mr. Stap stretched forth no assisting hand, paid no heed; he was still occupied with the registrar's certificate; reading over and over again the writing and the printing—trying, perchance, to detect some flaw in the document, to persuade himself that it had reference to a death or a birth, perhaps, not to a marriage. Vain effort! It was only too clear. Liz Moyle had become the wife of Herbert Gifford. He stared at the paper until his eyes were dim; the letters ran into each other, grew confused, and finally seemed to disappear altogether. He let the certificate glide from his fingers, and flutter away from him on to the floor.

"Who'd have thought it would have ended like this?" he said, tremulously. The remark was addressed apparently to the reflected image of himself in the glass over the mantelshelf.

"Mrs. Herbert Gifford's very good health," hiccuped the bride's father on the hearthrug. "Brayvo, Liz!"

"I might have known what was going on," Jemmy continued. "I knew she was a bad lot; that she wasn't to be depended upon; that every other word she uttered was a lie; but I didn't quite think it would come to this. I don't know what call she had to use me so bad. She might have told me plain that she didn't care for me, and not gone on fooling me as she has done. Why couldn't she have said straight out that she liked the other feller best? I could have borne that; I could have understood that."

"How you do go on muttering, Jemmy! Why can't you help me up, instead of turning round and round me like a horse at Ashley's? Fill your tumbler anyhow, my man, and drink Liz's health. Very good health—Mrs. Herbert Gifford—bride and bridegroom!"

"And I don't believe now that she really cares for him; she can't care for him—the white-faced sneak! That's what he is. It's his money that's tempted her; that's where he's had the pull of me. The rich are for ever trampling on the poor. But she ought to be ashamed of herself, that she ought. The way she's led me on, and fooled me, and not cared a bit for me all the time! Why, she's no more feeling—she hasn't—no—no more than that bottle!"

"'The bottle's the sun of our table,'" William Moyle began singing; "'Its beams are rosy wine!'" But a fit of coughing interrupted the bacchanal ditty.

"Where have they gone?" Mr. Stap demanded of his uncle.

"The happy pair," said William Moyle, with tipsy solemnity—punctuating his speech with hiccups—"the happy pair—have left town—for Dover—*en route*—for the Continent."

"I followed the cab as far as I could; but it was too fast for me; and I run against a post, and knocked all the breath out of my body. It's a shameful cruel business; no good will come of it—you mark my words." Mr. Stap assumed a grave prophetic air. "I say no good will come of it. It will end in shame and misery to all concerned. Good can't come of a thing that's been all lies, and treachery, and deceit, and—and" —he paused for a sufficiently strong expression— "cold-blooded hypocrisy and cowardice from the very beginning." He felt relieved by the explosive utterance of these vehement words; he went on in a milder tone: "However, I'm out of it now; there's that to be said. Perhaps I've cause to be grateful; I don't know as I haven't. It's all over, so far as I'm concerned. I've nothing more to do with it. I'm altogether out of it now." And, as though to give additional significance and force to this statement, he seized his hat, and abruptly quitted the room.

Mr. Moyle had closed his eyes, and appeared to be composing himself to sleep upon the rug as comfortably as circumstances would permit.

Jemmy was very angry; he was in a fever of excitement and indignation. It seemed to him there wasn't sufficient space to breathe in the confined parlour of his uncle's house. He felt the open night-air coolly refreshing and invigorating. He took off his hat, so that his heated forehead might have the full benefit of the breeze. And so, bareheaded, he walked up and down Whitfield Street, very wrathful, yet terribly sad and downcast. It could never be the same

Whitfield Street to him again. He thought how often he had come there, occupied with his courtship of his cousin Liz. What a splendid girl she was! Even in his anger against her, he could admit that. What eyes! what ringlets! what red lips! what ankles! what a figure altogether! He knew no one who could come any way near her. Mentally he ran through a list of female acquaintances.

"Why she beat 'em all by chalks," he cried, in a quavering tone. "Not one of 'em could touch her! A feller might well be proud to be seen with such a bit o' muslin on his arm."

But the "bit o' muslin" was lost to him for ever now—secured by his rival—and carried away to Dover by the night-train, *en route* for the Continent.

Disparagement followed quickly upon his praise. He took to very severe opinions of his cousin; just as a quick-tempered votary, in his disappointment that no particular result follows his prayers, rudely batters down the idol he was but now humbly bending before. He grew very abusive; he went over a long catalogue of ugly epithets, and fitted them all to his late mistress, Liz Moyle. And he was not very reasonable or consistent—angry people seldom are. Now he gave all the blame of Liz's going off to Herbert; now he attributed it wholly to the lady herself. Now it was Herbert's doing; he had tempted her with money; he had bought her with his costly presents; he had won her with the bait of a superior station and a wealthy marriage. No wonder the poor girl had been lured away from her home and her friends and the man who truly loved her, and whom no doubt she still truly loved in secret, if only her own heart could be read, or its dictates consulted. It was thus ever the children of the poor were wiled away to betrayal and ruin by the heartless rich, who had no thought but for their own disgraceful pleasures and infamous appetites! He had always been a Radical in his political opinions, so far as he had any—lawyers' clerks always are Radicals—but his views now became most sanguinary *sans culottes* in character. In his unreason, rating Herbert as a member of the aristocracy, Jemmy began to look forward to an upsetting of the Government as at present constituted, and to a general stringing-up of the British nobility to the lamp-posts in Tottenham Court Road. At that moment he would have cheerfully driven a tumbril full of peers to a guillotine in the Haymarket, or wherever else such an instrument of punishment might be set up.

Then he turned from the subject of Herbert and his misdoing—having thoroughly worried it—to give Liz a turn, and pour a fresh vial of wrath upon her head. It was all her doing, all—of course it was—from the very beginning; it was easy to see that with half an eye. She had laid a trap for that poor pitiful fool of a young Gifford, and caught him. Of course he was quite powerless in her hands: like a mouse in the claws of a cat. What could he do, when she had made up her mind to marry him? No doubt she had coaxed, and pampered, and flattered him, as she well knew how—the artful, designing, impudent, brazen-faced vixen! She had led him on, with her smiles, and nods, and winning glances, and crocodile's tears, until the poor idiot hardly knew whether he was standing upon his head or his heels. *He* run away with *her?* No, no; no such thing. He hadn't the pluck to do it; he hadn't the mind; though he might have found the money. It was all her doing—every bit. She had run away with him; she had made him marry her, and go off with her to France. The wicked, selfish, cruel, scheming hussy! She had planned it all from first to last, and given notice to the registrar, and carried her husband there almost against his will. *He* do it? Not he,

He didn't dare. Why, see how he hung back in the cab, shivering, and afraid to show his ugly, sickly, puny white face at the window; while Liz was sitting by his side, keeping a sharp eye on the luggage, as bold as brass, as cool as a cucumber, as though she were quite accustomed to getting married and going abroad twice a week! Why, she was no more ashamed of herself than that cat! (And here he broke off, to pursue a feline wanderer of the night a long way down the street, until the chase evaded him by a vigorous leap through some area-railings, and then from a cistern on to the pavement below.) She was a shameless, infamous, artful, wicked, etc., etc., and so on, *da capo*.

He had some slight acquaintance with Liz's friend, Miss Minns the dressmaker, whose name appeared on the registrar's certificate as one of the witnesses of the marriage. He found himself stopping in front of the house in which that lady resided. He went out into the road to look up at the window of her room on the second floor. It was late; but Miss Minns's candle was still burning: it was evident that she had not yet retired for the night. So he ventured to ring her bell—the second in a long file of bells at the doorpost, with a little zinc ticket over it inscribed with her name. He pulled the bell twice; and at last the light disappeared from the second floor, and presently illumined the semicircle of glass over the street door.

"Who wants *me* at this hour?" Miss Minns inquired.

The door was only opened to the extent of a few inches; it was, indeed, prudently secured by the chain.

Only half Miss Minns's countenance was visible as she said through the opening, mysteriously,

"Oh, it's you, is it, Mr. Stap? Wait a moment. Step into the passage, please."

And Jemmy was admitted.

Circumstances were not especially favourable to the appearance of Miss Minns. The passage was but dimly lit by a swaling inch of tallow candle in a large battered brass chamber-candlestick, shaped rather like a basin, and placed upon the lowest step of the flight of stairs in the background. Still there was sufficient light to reveal certain peculiarities in Miss Minns's toilet, which plainly affirmed that she had already commenced to retire for the night. That her dress was unfastened at the back, for instance, was clear, by the resolute manner in which she squared her elbows to prevent it slipping from her shoulders, and the anxiety with which she was continually tacking about to prevent her visitor having any other than a full-face view of her. Her hair was rather scanty in point of quantity, and a dull fawn in hue, and was neatly done up in such a number of curl-papers, that her head was quite speckled with them, and looked rather like one of those savoy cakes plentifully stuck about with almonds which are so much affected at evening-parties. She was small and thin, with a sallow complexion, white eyelashes, and pink eyelids. She spoke with a high, shrill voice, and a rather affected air, and had a way of shutting her eyes every now and then, and gaping, and bowing her head, as though she were taking numberless imaginary pills, which was a little alarming to bystanders until they became thoroughly accustomed to it. She seemed rather to gasp for breath as she spoke, which might arise in part from the haste with which she had come down-stairs, and in part from her anxiety to communicate with Mr. Stap, respecting her share in the marriage of his cousin.

"Anybody but you, Mr. Stap, of course I wouldn't have seen. No, certainly not, this hour of the night and all; of course it would never have done; but with you it's different. And indeed it was poor Liz—poor thing!"—and Miss Minns pronounced poor like *paw*—"her last words, that I should see you and explain, if I had the chance; and I hardly thought to have had so soon; though sooner or later, of course, you would come to hear of it, as was only natural; and it really can't matter which. And dear Liz, poor thing! desired me to say that she hopes you'll forgive her, and that her last thoughts on going off was of you; and think of you she always will, with loving-kindness, as a dear friend, who might have been something more if only Fate hadn't otherwise ordered, and Mr. G. been so determined. Poor thing! it was a dreadful trial to her; and I am sure I thought her heart it would have broke, and her tears flowed to that extent when she said good-bye to me, that it was well indeed she had a spare handkerchief. While for Mr. G., poor young man, he was that nervous, and timid, and upset, that you might have knocked him down with a teaspoon; and white as any sheet he was, I'm sure; for of course he had his feelings like anybody else, and a marriage is the tryingest of all things, no doubt; and this being clandestine made it worse a great deal, very likely, to both parties. Though of clandestine marriages I never did approve—no, Mr. Stap, nor never will; better all things open and above board, as I have always said. But what could *I* do? With dear Liz, poor thing! on her bended knees imploring me, and Mr. G. beseeching me dreadful; and I'd always promised dear Liz to be her bridesmaid, though in this clandestine way I never dreamt of it. But there, it's done now, and all the talking in the world won't undo it, though I will say it, a marriage before the *register* doesn't seem to me to be a marriage at all; if he had only worn a *surplus,* and looked ever so little like a minister, it would have been something; but no, not he, cool and sharp, with his pen behind his ear, and thinking no more of the importance of the thing than if he'd been selling a yard of tape behind a counter. And the bride looking no more like a bride than I do, poor thing! I'm sure, with my hair in papers and all—I don't know what you'll think of me, Mr. Stap; but I was just going to bed, and never gave a thought to your coming to-night—and not even in a book-muslin dress, poor dear! but in her plum-silk which I turned for her last winter, trimmed up the front with blue ribbon, and a real-lace hedging round the neck, and her figure looking lovely, as it always does. Her bonnet *was* new, a sweet pink, and in that I *did* contrive to slip ever so tiddy a slip of orange-blossom, hid under the bow at the side. And how we should ever have got on without Mr. Buckridge—I think his name was, but I didn"t quite ketch it (*"Buckhurst,"* Mr. Stap murmured, correcting her, but he was barely audible, and Miss Minns went on without heeding him)—the groomsman, a most genteel young man, but a wicked one, I'm sure; he nearly made me die of laughing with the things he said after the cirimony—the creecher—how would he like it himself? He kept us all up to the mark, and but for him I don't believe poor Mr. G. would have got through with it at all."

Jemmy Stap registered mentally a malediction upon Mr. Buckridge, otherwise Buckhurst, the groomsman.

"The turn it give me," Miss Minns continued, "when I heard a cab stop during the cirimony! But it was nothing; only a gent called to register the death of his wife; a bad omen, as I thought then, and think still; and dear Liz, poor thing! her breathing became that short, I thought it would have bust the seams of her dress. It was Mr. G.'s Pa as objected, I believe, to the match; so, Mr. Moyle, he couldn't do other than stay away, though of course the same objections don't apply in his case; and I'm sure I hope they'll be happy, though if every marriage was to be clandestine it would be a poor look-out indeed for the dressmakers. Poor dear! she had nothing that you could call a *trousseau*, and I'm sure her luggage was no more than if she'd been going to Margate for a week's bathing; but time was so short, you see, and Mr. G. so urgent, that there was no help for it. And I'd always looked forward to making dear Liz's bridal dress, and often and often, when she's been here to have a friendly cup of tea with me—and always kindly welcome she was, I'm sure—have I talked over her dress with her, and all but taken her order for it. And make it I did; but I little thought it would be that plum-silk I turned for her last winter, though it fitted her like a glove, it did, and became her complexion sweetly. And indeed I always thought as you was to be the happy man, Mr. Stap; but of course, what must be, must, as I always say; and what can't be, can't. But, poor dear! she hoped and prayed so that you would forgive her, and not take on about her marrying Mr. G., nor do nothing rash. And she hoped you'd soon find some one else to love you, and as you could love, and might be happy with for ever and ever. Amen." (Miss Minns spoke with quite religious fervour here.) "And as she said, poor thing! looking lovely the while, and the tears running down her cheeks—that she feared as you would have found her more expensive than you could have afforded, and that perhaps what had happened was, after all, the best for all parties. Good night, Mr. Stap; any time you're passing, shall of course be delighted, and a cup of tea always at five o'clock punctual, and sorry indeed it's too late to ask you up-stairs now, and to have kep you talking in the 'all all this time; but the neighbours must be considered; and such things as are now said about people for the veriest of trifles, it's quite shocking, and dreadful malicious. Good night. So glad you thought of ringing the bell. And don't be hard upon dear Liz, poor thing! was her last words, and so she begged me to say. Good night."

And Mr. Stap, not greatly consoled, left Miss Minns. He walked slowly home to Fetter Lane. He was very miserable. He quite marvelled at himself and the state of depression into which he had sunk. His humble lodging reached, he sat down on his bed, and with a shiver hid his face in his hands.

"I didn't think I should ever have felt so

shut up and miserable about anything, least of all about a woman," he said ruefully. "I know I never meant it. I liked Liz, confound her! but I didn't think I cared for her so much as this comes to."

Poor fellow! He had not imagined that love was a sort of speculation in which there is no limited liability. You may begin indifferently, with a small investment; but, sooner or later, your whole capital is pretty sure to be drawn into the business. Like playing with fire; you may deem that you are merely amusing yourself with a few sparks; but none the less you are running a dangerous risk of burning down your whole premises. He had intended that the "bit o' muslin" should simply hang on to his arm as a sort of external ornament more than anything else; but somehow it had shifted its position, and got fixed to his heart, winding round it with curious closeness and intricacy, so that it came away at last with an awful wrench and terrible pain.

Then he took a grim joy in kicking about the room and otherwise damaging the articles of hardware—great bargains—purchased in the New Cut, Liquorpond Street, and elsewhere, with a view to the change in his condition which could now never be. He continued this occupation until the lodger on the floor beneath knocked on the ceiling (with a poker, as it seemed) by way of hint that his rest was being disturbed by the noise, and he didn't like it. So Jemmy stopped.

"What a fool I am!" he said. And then the tears blinded him; and he went to bed. He was very angry; yet, let it be said of him, he never once thought of any deed of vengeance against the lady who had jilted him.

"Something's disagreed with you," observed Dawkins (Dashford's Common-Law) when Mr. Stap entered the lawyer's office on the following morning. Mr. Dawkins was a little mistaken; he dreamt that his young friend's stomach was disordered; but it was his heart. Perhaps the results of the two complaints are very similar.

"Do you want a job? Here's a *capias* out against a swell at the West End. You can go up with the sheriff's officer and help nab him, if you like. He's to be heard of at the Alcibiades Club; but you're more likely to catch him at his lodgings in Jasmin Street."

The name of the "swell at the West End" was the Honourable Clement Buckhurst.

"I'll go," said Jemmy promptly; "it will do me good."

And he proceeded westward with a large-nosed, snuffy, soiled gentleman, of the Jewish persuasion apparently; who was no bigot, however, for he consumed a pork-sausage roll, moistened by a pint of warm porter, with quite a Christian avidity and relish. Mr. Stap treated his companion to these choice refreshments.

"One thing," Mr. Stap said, with a hollow laugh, "I shall have more money to spend now. I've no call now to save up against my marriage. We'll have another pint, Boses" (this was addressed playfully to the Jewish gentleman), "after we've nabbed the swell."

He looked forward to the capture of Mr. Clement Buckhurst with some interest, not simply because that gentleman had done duty as a witness on the occasion of a late marriage before the registrar-general of St. Pancras; but Mr. Stap felt himself to be at war with the world generally; that relations of an amicable kind were absolutely suspended between society and himself; and he longed to rush into action, and strike a blow at somebody. It was a wonder he did not quarrel with the Jewish gentleman; but he perhaps felt that his companion was a sort of ally, equally at war with the rest of mankind. For the world does not entertain very kindly opinions concerning sheriff's officers, viewing them less in their real character as simple instruments of law and justice, than as a birds of prey and enemies of their species.

Very silent and sad, pale, with a look of suffering upon her face, and the traces of weeping about her eyes, Clare wandered from room to room of the house in Cumberland Crescent. She could find no occupation. Her embroidery—once lovod so dearly, with all its delicate intricacy of silks and gold and silver threads—had now lost its charms for her; her piano was untouched; once or twice she had tried to sing, but her voice gave way, breaking into sobs long before the end of her song was reached; even Sweep the kitten—that whilom darling—was neglected, missed many caresses and nursings, and luxurious breakfasts from the cream-jug. The poor girl moved about restlessly; could settle to nothing; pursued by sad thoughts, with a burden upon her heart that seemed to be greater than she could bear. She had never known trouble before; and this was no light one. Yet all sympathy was denied to her; there was no one to whispor in her ear words of hope or comfort; all were against her. She stood alone, fighting a hard fight with a foe so resolute, so powerful as Richard Gifford. Yet again and again she whispered to herself that she would sooner die than yield; that she would be true to the last to Noel Tredgold.

Mrs. Gifford, stretched upon her couch in the drawing-room, warding off the light with her feather fan, watched her daughter with frightened eyes. She grew sick with alarm as she noted the change in her, as she considered each incident of her struggle with Richard Gifford. Her love for Clare gave the poor timid woman courage at last. She plucked up heart enough to say gently to her husband,

"Have you noticed Clare lately? She is really ill."

"A little pale; she will soon be better," Mr. Gifford answered.

"Yet, if she really wishes it—I'm sure I would not oppose her for the world—why should she not marry this man, if she really loves him, if he really loves her in return? She has money enough for both."

"It is impossible."

"I am sure Clare would do nothing unworthy. With her fortune she has some claim to please herself in her marriage. If this Mr.——"

"Let me hear no more on this subject," Mr.

Gifford said, sternly. "Clare must be protected against herself. She is capable of an act of romantic folly. But it must not be; I have already chosen a husband for her. She must marry Herbert."

"Herbert!"

"You will be kind enough to exert all your influence to accomplish that object. It is imperatively necessary. The sooner the marriage can take place, the better for all concerned."

Mr. Gifford spoke in a sharp, incisive manner, and then turned away, as though there was nothing more to be said upon the subject.

"I thought of Clement Buckhurst; I never dreamt of Herbert," Mrs. Gifford said, faintly. "I don't think Clare will ever consent."

"*She must.* By the way, where *is* Herbert? I have not seen him this day or two; and I've been so occupied and harrassed with other things——"

Where *was* Herbert? He was not to be found. No one knew anything about him. He had absented himself from the house a good deal lately. He had gone, and left no trace. Yes, something was left—a letter for Clare. It contained an enclosure addressed to his father.

CHAPTER VI.

MONEY-MARKET AND CITY INTELLIGENCE.

"THINGS are very queer in the City, very queer indeed."

So old Zachary Moyle mumbles over and over again, as he sits curved up, toasting his toes and knees before the kitchen fire in Whitfield Street, watching the burning coals, with an eye now and then for the legs passing the area-railings, working out in his mind—so he describes his mental occupation—the events happening around him, as though they were sums on a slate. But his calculations crowd upon him, and somehow he cannot make them come right so quickly as he used to do. He admits that he is not the man he was; his cough troubles him greatly at times; and he speaks more and more often now of the great difficulties, when he is in a recumbent position, in the way of drawing his breath. There are things going on about him he cannot understand. His son William's presence in the house, for instance, during the hours formerly devoted to Messrs. Fordyce and Fordyce and the City. No word of the quarrel with Mr. Gifford has reached him. Indeed, William Moyle seldom enters the kitchen now; it may be to avoid all discussion with the old man touching the great change that has taken place, or because a secret tavern he has lately discovered in the neighbourhood, and now visits constantly at all hours of the day, affords him more enjoyment and a greater variety of drinks than he can obtain in his own house. Liz too is away; and his grandson Jemmy never comes near Whitfield Street now. Poor old Zachary cannot understand it; and there is no one to assist him to an explanation. He is left wholly to the care of Nance—who is equal to the charge, be it said, and takes a pride in her toil in behalf of the old man; but who still regards him something too much in the light of a pet dog, or cat, or bird, and who will nod and smile, sing and talk nonsense to him by the hour together, but is quite incapable of giving him any lucid interpretation of the mysteries that are bewildering him. So the doings in Whitfield Street day by day pass more and more beyond the limits of his comprehension; and at last, just as a child over-puzzled with a long sum sets down a purely fanciful array of figures, and tries to make believe that the correct answer is found and the task accomplished, so old Zachary ends by persuading himself that he has discovered a satisfactory solution of the difficulties he is labouring under, and avers that "It's all along of things being queer in the City." He attributes everything to this; and makes believe that he is quite content and at ease now upon the subject. Of course he understands the explanation no more than he understands the mystery; but he sets the one vagueness against the other, makes them balance, and closes the account.

"It's things being queer in the City. Yes, that's what it is; things being queer in the City;" and so on, mumbling the words over and over again.

And now a thousand echoes seem to take up the tale. The same mysterious words are heard to issue from many other lips than poor old Zachary's. It seems to be quite the talk of the world, this same strange fact, that things are queer in the City. The air seems quite heavy, as with thunder, it reverberates so with the incessant repetitions of these words. Men meeting in the street are fain to speak at once of the queerness of things in the City, even before they have made mention of the state of the weather, the quarter of the wind, or inquired concerning each other's bodily condition of health. And yet it is probable that the majority of the speakers upon the subject can boast little more real enlightenment in regard to it than is possessed by poor old Zachary Moyle, retired market-gardener, crouching over the kitchen-fire in Whitfield Street. Like him, they know that matters of great importance are somehow wrapped up in those words; but further they cannot go; the length and breadth and depth of that importance they know nothing about, and can in no way define or comprehend. For "the City" is an enormous mystery; and the initiated are very reticent, or are without the faculty of imparting information. Outsiders can but gape and wonder and listen, repeating what they hear: syllables of an oracular sound, and a most vague significance.

The cause and origin of commercial crises, who will be bold enough to trace out and declare? It is possible that they are governed by particular laws—as are eclipses, earthquakes, and other natural phenomena; and to financial *savans*—there are such people—they may seem simple and normal matters enough. But to the unlearned, the panic that appears on a sudden, like a ghost, on the money-market, frightening the merchants and the money-dealers from their propriety, will ever seem a something strange and very wonderful. The cry of *sauve qui peut* is heard, and pell-mell flight and confusion ensue, as matters of course. Men fling down their arms, desert their colours, and sometimes their country, and leave all sorts of stores and baggage and treasures upon the field. Everywhere is ruin and bankruptcy and desolation. All this may of course be wholly unavoidable. I am speaking as one lamentably uninformed upon the subject. For all I know to the contrary, a panic is one of those ills the City is heir to, and cannot elude. A crisis is an inevitable malady of commerce, just as the measles are of man; and "business" must expect these epileptic sort of seizures, and progress as best it may in spite of them. But certainly the City seems to gain little by its former experiences of the same kind. The panic comes: its effect is just as marvellous and alarming this time as the last; it is just as new and horrible and unexpected as if it had never been known before; yet there have been two or three periods of monetary convulsion within the knowledge of the present generation; they are matters of history, and their recurrence is seemingly a matter of some regularity, and, one would think, might be calculated upon and prepared for in some way. However, this, it seems, is never done, or thought worth doing.

As yet, however, the panic is not. There is firing in the distance; the crack of it can be heard distinctly, is matter of notoriety; but it may be only a little skirmishing in the extreme front, or simply a trifling affair of outposts. Certainly the main body of the financial army are not engaged; they are reposing on their arms quietly enough, out of the reach of danger, apathetic rather than anxious; for no one appears to expect that anything serious is likely to come of the smoke upon the horizon, that "earnest" is meant, than an advance of the whole line will speedily become necessary, and a general engagement of a most desperate character involve the entire force. But the firing is drawing nearer. Some combatants are perceptibly paling and clenching their teeth. Some are already looking eagerly towards the rear in the direction of the supports. Men are dropping rather quickly on the outer fringe of the army, and now and then a shell finds it way to the centre and deals out destruction rather liberally. The articles on City intelligence in the *Times* furnishes a daily list of disasters and casualties. Stoppages at Rio, at Valparaiso, at Singapore, at Smyrna, and elsewhere, have been noted. A regiment of hard-named Greek merchants have gone down, as at a blow, after a very slight resistance. Many colonial strongholds have surrendered. Numberless reputed strong men have succumbed. General officers are carried from the field grievously hurt; heads of houses are lying low: the excitement spreads and intensifies; the noise is tremendous; men can hardly hear themselves speak. The action has become universal; it is all-absorbing; men who deemed themselves far away, quite out of range, secure from harm, mere spectators, are soon drawn in, deeply involved. The battle rages; the reserves are employed—are already exhausted. The panic is now very near indeed.

Mr. Gifford sits at his desk in the office of the old firm of Fordyce and Fordyce, near the Bank of England. Letters and papers crowd round him; there is hardly an available inch of clear space upon his desk; quite a spring-tide of documents has come in, surrounding him, overflowing his table, and littering the floor. It seems just now in the nature of things that spring-tides of documents should be surging up in City-offices, threatening to swamp City men. Every counting-house is similarly situated. These great financial battles are carried on, as it were, with paper pellets, which inflict most mortal wounds notwithstanding. A sheet or two of bank-post paper from a long distance, delivered calmly by the postman at the office-door, brings down for ever very noble City celebrities at an instant's warning. Great houses collapse with a frightful crash, as though a torpedo had been fired in the cellars beneath them. A man thousands of miles off effects ruin at home, as though he had despatched an electric spark along a hidden wire communicating with a mine beneath his correspondent's desk. Letters and papers litter the City; they are as the cartridges which strew the battle-field—where they lie the thickest, there, be sure, the battle has raged the most fiercely.

At a first glance, perhaps, you might think that Mr. Gifford looked nearly as calm and unmoved as ever he had done. For he withstood change very well. He had an habitual gravity of manner, was always solemn and stately, thin and pale, with a certain rigidity of features which effectually prevented any great variety of expression from appearing in his face. But examining him more carefully, you would be soon struck with the notion that he had aged very much of late. His body was still erect; but his head drooped forward, so that his shoulders seemed to have risen, and his chin was nearly resting on his chest. And of late the fringe of iron-grey hair at the back of his head had become quite white; the dark sallowness of his complexion had faded to an unhealthy paleness; his eyes had dulled, were now lustreless, sunken; his thinness approached emaciation; there was a slight tremble about his hands; and in the hollow of his cheeks there was a restless, nervous pulsing.

Before him lay Herbert's letter: he had read and read it repeatedly; he must have pretty well learnt it by heart at last. He had thrust it back into its envelope each time after perusing it. And now he was making notes upon the envelope; his gold pencil-case was jotting down lines upon lines of figures. He turned to consult other papers near him, and then set to work adding more and more figures; and then he would pause and gaze at the fireplace in front of him, with an air of painful abstraction. He next took up a legal-looking paper, something like a counsel's brief—many closely-written sheets, tied together at the top, at the left-hand corner, with red tape.

By the endorsement on the outer sheet, it appeared that this was a copy of the settlement made on the marriage of the Honourable Ferdinand Edward Augustus Gray and Clare Adelaide Clinton. The deed bore date more than twenty years back.

It was under this settlement, we may here note, that Clare Gray derived her fortune. She was the only issue of the marriage. Upon the death of her father, the Honourable Ferdinand Edward Augustus Gray, as the reader has been already apprized, his widow, formerly Miss Clinton, had married Richard Gifford, a widower with one son, Herbert. The trustees of this deed had been selected to hold that office apparently for the reasons that appear generally to rule in the matter of the choice of trustees. They were people remarkably unaccustomed to business affairs; and they were all of so advanced an age, that it was extremely unlikely they would survive to carry out the provisions of the trusts they were charged with. They were originally four in number, and were divided in character, as is also usual in such cases, between trustees of inflexible nature, who were so impressed with the importance of their duties that they would consent to nothing, and trustees of easy nature, who thought lightly of their labours, and would consent to anything. Under these circumstances, it was, of course, quite a mercy that the settlement had been kept out of Chancery: that Clare was not made a ward of court, and the victim of that most unfriendly of proceedings—a "friendly suit." It was said that it had been only the interposition of Mr. Gifford that had saved his step-child from such a fate. Mr. Gifford was, however, assisted by death; for two of the trustees, the most preposterous of the four, had been relieved at their posts by that "fell sergeant" while the settlement was but a young deed, and its parchment of quite a fair and delicate complexion. It had grown wrinkled and sallow enough since. No new trustees had been appointed in the room of those removed; and quite lately, another, who had been lunatic for some years, had departed. So that now, one only was left surviving—a genial old clergyman (the others had been all military men, excellent trustees for home affairs, because they were nearly always abroad, in command of foreign stations), a West-of-England rector, of extreme age, who was profoundly ignorant of his duties; who never had been able to comprehend why he had been made trustee at all, though he felt it somehow as a compliment, like having his health proposed at the wedding breakfast (he had assisted the bishop who joined the hands of Mr. and Mrs. Gray at the altar), and who came up to town quarterly to have his hair cut, to see his wine-merchant, and to say what enormous confidence he had in Mr. Gifford, and that to him he left all the business arrangements of the trusteeship. Of this worthy old gentleman it may further be said, that he took great pride in his signature—it was certainly a good one—and was fond of affixing it, upon the slightest provocation, to anything that was put before him or that came in his way. But there: he is not the only man whoso only chief notion of business consists in readiness to give a signature when asked; or, indeed, oftentimes when not asked so to do.

With this excellent old gentlemen Mr. Gifford had had considerable correspondence. The rector wrote good letters, and knew that he did so. They were a little wordy, but admirable English. The older he grew, the fonder he became of his letter-writing. He had not much else to do. He had been very many years in his rectory, during which time he had cured all the few souls about him very thoroughly, and so had leisure. He wrote more and more to Mr. Gifford; and in one of his letters he mentioned, incidentally, that he was aware Miss Clare Gray would soon be of age.

Among other papers, Mr. Gifford had been examining some recent letters from his correspondent, the rector, in the west.

"I hope the old man is not going to give trouble. Can anybody have got hold of him, and put him up to asking questions? It's very provoking; at this time of all others."

And then he went over again the figures on the back of Herbert's letter. Then he looked at his watch.

"I am only losing time," he said.

It was about noon; yet he had been some hours at his desk: for some weeks past he had been early and late at his office.

"Strange," he said, as he rose, "I feel quite giddy—from getting no rest last night, I suppose."

For a moment he seemed to breathe with difficulty, and pressed his hand upon his left side. He quite recovered himself, however, presently, and went out; he got into a hansom cab, and told the cabman to drive to Whitfield Street, Tottenham-Court Road.

He found William Moyle at home; he was sitting in the parlour, smoking, and sipping what looked like plain water; but it was really something rather stronger. There was a scent as of spirits about the room, which there was no mistaking. Mr. Gifford ordered the cab to wait.

William Moyle rose and bowed as his late employer entered the room.

"I thought it possible I might have the honour of seeing you, Mr. Gifford." He spoke nervously—was indeed a little frightened. Yet he wore a certain air of triumph.

"I have here a letter from my son," Mr. Gifford began, sternly, abruptly. "It seems he has left the country in company with your daughter."

"She is his wife."

"He says so. Don't trouble yourself"—for the other was fumbling in his pocket, and produced the registrar's certificate—"I will take for granted that it is as he says. No doubt, as a father, you have been careful that your daughter left you as a wife, rather than in a less reputable character. So far your scheme has been successful, and I congratulate you. I am beaten, I admit it. I underrated my son's capacity for folly, or rather, perhaps, should say I overrated his honesty."

"Young people will be young people," William Moyle said, with a smile. "What's done can't be helped. It's no use being angry now, all the mischief's over."

Mr. Gifford's gesture signified impatience and contempt.

"It was not this matter brought me here, or at least not this branch of it. My son has made his bed, and he may lie in it; though it may prove that he has made it in a felon's prison."

William Moyle started.

"You don't mean to say, Mr. Gifford——"

"My son, your daughter's husband, has raised money by fraudulent means. He has forged the acceptance of the firm to bills for various sums. You knew of this?"

"I—I would rather not say whether I had any notion of this or not. But I suppose he found he couldn't go abroad without money. He reckoned upon your admitting him to partnership very shortly, and has been a little premature perhaps, and indiscreet. Such things have happened before now. But what of that?"

"He will take the consequences," Mr. Gifford said, quietly.

William Moyle was incredulous. He laughed; but it was rather a frightened, foolish sort of laugh, when he found the stern face before him did not move a muscle; when the fixed eyes that gazed into his did not blink; when no one sign of relenting was to be perceived in the grim, calm man confronting him.

"You can't mean it, sir. You can't know what you're saying." He spoke breathlessly—in jerks. "Your own son, Mr. Gifford; a boy in years—a mere boy. Your *only* son."

"And your son-in-law. Don't let us forget that."

"And this amount—a mere trifle; a few poor pounds to pay his expenses abroad."

"A trifle, you call it!" Mr. Gifford interrupted. "You talk like a millionnaire or a chancellor of the exchequer. It's for lack of such trifles as these that houses in the City are now stopping payment. In such a time as this one has no money to throw away; no such thing now as a balance lying idle. For every pound in one's possession there is a hand stretched out. A sovereign to spare is almost more than one can count on. I tell you, the last ounces of the load are being laid on, and the camels' backs are breaking—breaking every hour. No one is safe; no one can answer for himself. If my own house is solvent, it is more than I know."

He had raised his voice, and was speaking with some violence. He stopped, to press his side, and pass his handkerchief across his forehead.

"And you expect me to provide suddenly for such *trifles* as this?" he said, bitterly.

He held before William Moyle the envelope of Herbert's letter, pointing to a particular line of figures.

"It's not *that* amount? it can't be!" William Moyle started back with a scream of alarm. Then, as though talking to himself, he continued: "He said something of play-debts—debts of honour he called them—due to Mr. Buckhurst——"

"I begin to understand the matter better now," Mr. Gifford said, in a low voice.

There was silence for some time.

"You won't be hard upon him, Mr. Gifford," William Moyle urged tremulously. "Think how young he is; and have some pity for him!"

"Did you show any consideration for his youth, and his folly, and his weakness, when you laid your snares for him, and tricked him into a disgraceful marriage with your trumpery daughter? Understand me, Moyle. *You* began this contest with me; it shall go on now to the end. Herbert Gifford was no longer a son of mine when he became your son-in-law. He is now simply a forger and a thief. He has tried to rob me; perhaps not me so much as the creditors of my firm. Well, I have done with him. I hand him over to the law. I go from here to the police-office, to give information of the forgery. He will be pursued and brought back. You may expect to see him in England again very shortly, standing in the felon's dock, to answer the charge which I shall bring against him. Be sure *I* shall not flinch; do not think it for a moment. If I keep my word in nothing else, I swear to you that I will keep it in this."

William Moyle answered with a groan. He bowed his head over the table, so that his face was hidden, and clasped his hands at the back of his neck. Mr. Gifford rose.

"I thought it right to inform you of the course I intended to pursue in regard to the gentlemen who has so recently become a member of your family. Upon reflection, you will perhaps consider that altogether it would have been possible for your daughter to have made a more eligible match; that it would have been better if she had been less ambitious—had married some one of her own rank and station, and, above all, an honest man."

Some one burst hurriedly into the room.

"We've took him. He was caught last night. He would have settled and got out this morning; but the other creditors got wind of it, and the detainers came in in swarms. So he moves on from Cursitor Street to the Bench this afternoon."

Jemmy Stap was the speaker. The two men turned towards him inquiring eyes.

"The Honourable Clement Buckhurst, I mean," said Mr. Stap, apprehending that some explanation was necessary. Seeing Mr. Gifford, he went on: "I beg your pardon, sir; I thought my uncle was alone."

Mr. Gifford nodded, smiled curiously, and went out without saying another word.

"Where to?" asked the cabman.

"Back to the City."

And the cab rattled away.

He did not return immediately, however, to the office of Messrs. Fordyce and Fordyce. Nor did he proceed to the police-office to give information of the forgery, as he had promised William Moyle that he would do. He stopped at his banker's, in one of the narrow side-streets twisting out of Lombard Street. It was called a "lane," and was indeed quite a City green lane; for it boasted two or three pretty lively lime-trees, in a little enclosure, which might be a burial-ground or a private garden, it was hard to say which; and it possessed also a City church—the inside of which no man had ever seen—with a projecting clock, like an old public-house sign, or as though it were hung out for sale, while in the hurry of business it had been forgotten to mark the price on it in plain figures.

He entered the banker's, passing the long counter where the cashiers, with a sort of brisk apathy, stood all day long shovelling gold out in copper scoops to the presenters of cheques.

He went past this counter to the sacred precincts beyond. He found himself among a tribe of elderly functionaries with bald heads, in a region intersected by mahogany screens and green-silk curtains, with private parlours in the distance. He was received, not with ceremony for they are not ceremonious in banking establishments, but still with some deference. Fordyce and Fordyce were old customers; their connection with the bank had extended over a very long course of years; they were an extremely respectable house, and Mr. Gifford was now their representative—stood in their shoes, so to speak, so far as the bank was concerned. The visitor soon found himself closeted with a bland, clean, rather wise-looking gentleman of middle age, whose occupation seemed to be all day long to lean with his back against a marble mantelpiece summer and winter, and inform people who came to see him upon all sorts of propositions, that, "Really now, he thought the bank could do it;" or, "Really now, he thought the bank couldn't do it," just as the case might happen.

To Mr. Gifford, whatever his proposal, the last form of answer was given, with polite sadness; but yet it was evident peremptorily. "Really now, he thought the bank couldn't do it," said the bland gentleman of middle age. And it seemed to be understood that the answer was quite conclusive; still the two men went on talking, as though it were but a trifling matter of business between them, of no real moment. The times were dreadful, quite dreadful; things in the City were in that state; Mr. Gifford had seen the leader in the paper of that morning? It had done a great deal of mischief, unquestionably it had. In the present excited condition of men's minds, the smallest things had an extraordinary effect. Mr. Gifford had heard the news this afternoon? No? not what the Bank had done? No? Nor the strange proceedings on the Bourse? No? There were the latest quotations. Such sudden falls were almost unprecedented; it was very hard indeed to account for them in any satisfactory way. And then there were more failures; more and more failures. Only just now he had learnt of the stoppage of So-and-So's old-established East-Indian house, through over-dealing of the Calcutta branch with the paper of that confounded Cochin-China Banking Company—one of the oldest houses in the City. It was most extraordinary. A had gone too, and B, and C, with a crash. There could only be the veriest trifle of a dividend. Poor D had been let in frightfully. It behoved men to be very careful; to distribute their liabilities. Nothing was so bad, so dangerous, as putting all your eggs in one basket. Mr. Gifford would be quite surprised if he only knew the paper they had but that morning, within the last few minutes, declined to have anything to do with—some of the best names in the City. But no; the bank appreciated the danger of its position. It was not possible to be too careful just now. They had determined to adopt a very strict course, and to adhere to it rigidly (he came back here to Mr. Gifford's proposal). He had the greatest respect for Fordyce and Fordyce; but the bank had reached, if indeed it had not already exceeded, the limits it had prescribed to itself. Yes, there was so much already on F. and F.'s paper; so much on the title-deeds of the estate in Hampshire; so much on the lease of the house in Cumberland Crescent—it was a large sum altogether. "Really now, he thought the bank couldn't do it." And they parted in the most friendly way; they were quite laughing as the bland gentleman of middle age showed Mr. Gifford out of the private parlour. And then the bland gentleman leant again with his back against the marble mantelshelf, and tried to look as if nothing had happened, and he didn't think that things were very queer indeed with the old firm of F. and F.

"What to do?" Mr. Gifford asked himself, with a sort of gasp, as he sunk back in his cab. The cab had waited for him; the cabman enjoying himself immensely, eating nuts, while for full twenty minutes he effectually blocked up the City green lane with his vehicle, and converted it into a "no thoroughfare," to the impotent rage of a long line of carts and coaches, vans and trucks, etc.

Mr. Gifford was next taken to an insurance office, not far off; a gorgeous stucco edifice, with a tall flight of stone steps. Mr. Gifford had an interview with the secretary. Mr. Gifford was well known at the insurance office. He was one of its auditors, with a certainty of mounting to a seat at its direction at the first vacancy. His life was insured to a large amount. He proposed an advance from the company upon an assignment of his policy, a bond of indemnity, further charges upon his freehold estate in Hants and the house in Cumberland Crescent, of which he possessed a long lease. The secretary pondered a little, made a calculation upon his blotting-paper, then thought it possible the directors might entertain the proposal; thought it, indeed, very likely; especially considering the position which Mr. Gifford occupied in regard to the company. But was certain of one thing—the directors would require further insurance. (*Mem.* The directors were always insisting upon insurance; they made it a condition of every bargain they struck, every advance they made. It looked well in their annual report to say that so many thousands—or millions, as the case might be—of new policies had been issued during the past year.) Mr. Gifford agreed to make no difficulty about further insurance. Then if Mr. Gifford had no objection, it might be as well, perhaps, to get over that part of the business at once? It was a necessary preliminary. The medical officer of the company was still in attendance; would Mr. Gifford step into Dr. Moxon's room for a few minutes? the examination was a mere form, but it was absolutely indispensable. Mr. Gifford would see Dr. Moxon, and was forthwith ushered into the presence of that distinguished physician by a very tall, and very broad, and altogether a very magnificent porter, with a crimson face, and a scarlet waistcoat edged with gold lace—the waistcoat only, not the face; *that* was handsomely edged with thick auburn whiskers, except at the top, which was bald.

Dr. Moxon had been amusing himself with a glass or so of very dry sherry and a biscuit. He was now standing up by the window, performing a dexterous operation on his finger-nails with a sharp pen-knife. Dr. Moxon had some acquaintance with Mr. Gifford, and shook hands with him. They interchanged a few sentences about the weather, "things in the City"—that universal topic—and then proceeded to the business before them. Dr. Moxon had no doubt they could soon get through that. It was some years, he thought, since he had examined Mr. Gifford with a view to insurance? And he had never had a day's illness since. Well, come, that was very encouraging. The doctor wished he could say the same of himself.

Your tongue? Thank you. Your pulse? Much obliged. Now, does that hurt you? No. Does that? The doctor questions, and talks, and taps, and listens. But gradually a change takes place in his manner. It is still cheery and friendly, but it has lost that indifferent "matter-of-form" sort of air that at first distinguished it. He grows more particular and precise; he is evidently taking extreme pains with his examination —extraordinary pains, as it would seem. There is quite an anxious look upon his face as he throws open Mr. Gifford's waistcoat, and listens closely at his left side.

"That will do, thank you," he says; and he stands a little way off, fingering his chin, as though he rather fancied he might have cut himself while shaving, and was feeling about for the place.

"All right, doctor?" Mr. Gifford inquires, buttoning his waistcoat leisurely.

"Well, do you know, I think I must defer my report for the present. I think I must ask you to let this matter of further insurance stand over for a few weeks. I don't find you quite the thing. Don't be alarmed. I dare say it's nothing. Come again to me, say the month after next. Meanwhile, I think I would recommend repose, country air, very moderate diet, sedative medicine, and considerable depletion."

"It's very important to me to complete this business with the company," Mr. Gifford said. "I should not object to pay an increased premium, if you think there is greater risk in my case than ordinary."

"I don't say that, but——"

"You can speak plainly, Dr. Moxon."

"Upon the report I should now make, the company would, to a certainty, refuse the insurance."

Mr. Gifford waited a few moments.

"Thank you," he said quietly. "I have had some suspicions in regard to my state of health, but only very recently. Pray tell me, is there any immediate danger? I am a plain man of business. I have many things to do. It is important that I should be informed of the exact state of the case."

"You've a good nerve, Mr. Gifford. I congratulate you upon it. It's so much in your favour. But you must not alarm yourself needlessly. You know, I may be mistaken. I am far from speaking positively. I don't say for certain that there is aneurismal hypertrophy; but I think it possible there may be. The sounds produced by percussion are dull; the pulsations are remarkably strong; the sounds I detect by auscultation are louder than I like. Hypertrophy of the left ventricle frequently results in appoplexy and hæmorrhage. I won't say any more. Take care of yourself; avoid exertion as much as possible, and all exciting influences. But don't get frightened. We doctors, you know, are not infallible. And I think, if I were you, I'd get out of town; a quiet seaside place, not too bracing—let us say South Devon. I'm rather inclined to recommend Dawlish myself. Good-bye. Come again in a few weeks, and we'll see what we can do about this insurance. Good-bye."

"As pretty a case of that kind of thing as I think ever came under my notice," said the doctor, as he helped himself to another glass of dry sherry.

Mr. Gifford had gone.

"I might have guessed it," he said in a low voice, arrived again at his office, and once more at his desk and papers. "There was little need for me to wonder what this strange feeling here was"—he pressed his hand upon his side—"I, who remember my father, and how he died, with what terrible suddenness, and what the doctors said was the cause of death. I was a mere child at the time; long ago, now, long, long ago. Yet I remember it—how well!"

Then, after a long pause—

"The worst may come, then. It is out of my hands now. Yet one thing they must say of me—I have done all that was possible for Fordyce and Fordyce. They must do me that justice. I have paid a price to have that said."

CHAPTER VII.

THE LAURELS.

MEANWHILE the Honourable Clement Buckhurst was very angry indeed, biting his nails in a sponging-house, the captive of Messrs. Gashford, of Gray's Inn, at the suit of one of his numberless creditors. He walked up and down the sheriff's officer's "coffee-room" in Cursitor Street, breathing close, unwholesome atmosphere, resulting from the fumes of bad tobacco and indifferent brandy. And now he would go up to the window, and look out scowling through the bars, as though vaguely expecting to see some one coming to his relief. Now he would turn away with an oath, and drum upon the table with his clenched fists, or beat impatiently upon the floor with his feet.

"How cursed unlucky!" he said. "If I had but gone yesterday, as I had intended! But I stayed humouring every whim of that infernal jabbering idiot, Clotilde" (he alluded possibly to the lady dressed in the latest French fashions, with the artificially rosy cheeks and the chalk-white shoulders, in whose company he had been fond of publicly exhibiting himself of late, to the scandal of society); "and now it's come to this! Little enough she'll care. I may make oath of that."

And he laughed bitterly, and swore, stamped, and bit his nails, pulled at his moustache, and looked very white and wicked, ugly and unpleasant altogether.

"It's all U-P with me," he went on. "They've got me now, and they'll keep me; and I can't do anything. Old Alf's away; and I've quarrelled with him. Even if he were here, I doubt if he could or would do anything. He's no money, of course; but he might, if I'd kept him in a good humour, have gone round to these fellows and made terms with them, or got time for me, or something. But that can't be now. He's thrown me over, confound him. As for Beauflower or the Mater, they're out of the question; they're too far off; and if they were nearer, they'd do nothing; or they'd give me some tracts to read, and say I'd brought it on myself, and that it was a valuable lesson, and the best thing that could happen to me; and now I had time to see the error of my ways, they'd hope I'd repent and amend; and so on. It's infernally unlucky!"

He had money, of course. A great part of the plunder produced by his nefarious dealings with Herbert yet remained. But still his liabilities were very large. For years he had paid no one. His bill transactions had been on a ruinous scale. He had been in the habit of raising money at any price; and the claims against him were enormous. He was quite willing to throw a tub to the whale, as he termed it; but the whale declined to be satisfied with a tub. He would have paid off the first, and the second, and the third detaining creditors willingly, if he could have thus secured his liberty. But the whole body of his duns had been roused; they had got scent of what was going on, and satisfied themselves that now or never was the time for spirited action on their part; and they came down upon him with wonderful unity of purpose; they combined their forces, and their battle-cry was, "All, or none. Pay, or go to prison." Under these circumstances, Clem put his back to the wall and stood at bay. He determined to pay no one. Arrived at this conclusion, he brightened a little.

"I'll go the Bench," he declared. "It's

waste of time and money stopping here. It's the dead time of year. Perhaps people won't hear of it much. I believe a man can get on comfortably enough in the Bench if he's got money; and I'm pretty well off for the present in that respect. I'll tire these fellows out. They'll lower their tone when they find they can get nothing by it. A few weeks' time, and they'll be glad to let me out on my own terms."

So he quitted Cursitor Street, and was removed to the Queen's Bench Prison in the Borough, where he made himself as comfortable as he could, found several people he had known formerly, who had disappeared suddenly from society, no one knew why precisely, resumed his acquaintance with these, and took to the game of rackets very kindly.

Mr. Gifford had congratulated his discharged clerk upon the successful issue of his scheming. Yet William Moyle, in the parlour in Whitfield Street, with his head bowed over the table, so that his face was hidden, and his hands clasped at the back of his neck, did not appear an especially fit subject for congratulations. Still he had succeeded; his plans had been carried out to the letter; he had married his daughter—

his "trumpery daughter," Mr. Gifford had called her—to his employer's son: he had achieved a splendid match for her—"like Dick Whittington, only upside-down ways," as old Zachary had described it; he had triumphed; and yet how utterly miserable he was!

At first, perhaps, there had been some vagueness, if not some timidity, about his plans. He had not been slow to perceive the advantage that would result from entangling Herbert Gifford in an engagement to marry Liz; and he rejoiced inwardly and in secret as he took note that this end was being reached without any movement on his part. He had simply to let things take their course; his utmost aspiration at that time being to secure a considerable amount by way of compensation for the breach of engagement, which he made sure would ultimately ensue. But he did not sufficiently rely upon Herbert's infatuation or Liz's cleverness, which both pointed to marriage. He was a cautious, easily-frightened man, wholly without principle—his only child took after him in that respect—with certain mechanical, plodding habits, which gave some value to his services in the City. He had no ambition for himself; he would have been content to have gone on to the end a merchant's clerk, secure of his pipe, his grog, his mutton-chops, and his home near Tottenham-Court Road, if only his growing intemperance had permitted him. But still he was pleased with the thought that his child should soar beyond his humble station; he was proud of her—loved her in his way. So he accepted with eagerness at last the notion of her advantageous marriage, not the less pleased because he had now, as he fancied, a wrong to avenge. He had been discharged at a moment's notice. And he longed to punish and humiliate his master. The marriage promised an effectual method of effecting this. The mistake he had made arose from his own want of conscience and honesty. To him, Herbert's method of providing funds seemed a misdeed certainly, but still one of a very trivial nature, which could not possibly be judged harshly, or punished in any way. Even now he had some difficulty in comprehending, could not readily credit, Mr. Gifford's stern views of his son's fraudulent conduct. Certainly, thanks to Clement Buckhurst, Herbert had dealt with the name of his father's firm to an extent far beyond William Moyle's anticipations; and that might make some difference. Still he asked, Could Mr. Gifford possibly mean to proceed with rigour against his son? Would he bring such a disgrace upon himself and upon his family? He had declared that he would. But would he? That was the question. Then William Moyle remembered how cold, and hard, and cruel Mr. Gifford was, and hope seemed to die out of him. With raised hands he moaned out,

"My poor child, Liz! my poor child! Who would have dreamt of its ending like this!"

He had dismissed his nephew Jemmy with some violence and abruptness. Mr. Stap, it appeared, had not been moved with any great sympathy for Herbert's misfortunes; had not condoled much concerning the disappointment likely to follow so closely upon Liz's splendid marriage. Jemmy had even gone so far as to declare, with some approach to glee, "That it served them both jolly well right, and that he wasn't sorry. And that now they might have some notion as to what his feelings were on the subject, and would know generally what disappointment was like." After which announcement his uncle flung a tumbler at him, made a promising attempt at strangling him, and finally drove him from the house.

So he sat alone, terribly cast down, incapable of any effort, whimpering over the success of his schemes, rocking himself to and fro, lamenting the fate of his child. He knew not what to do. What would avail any attempt of his to inform Herbert of his danger? The police would be too quick for him. And probably the next thing he heard would be Herbert's arrest. And he shrunk with horror as he pictured to himself Liz's husband handcuffed, and brought in close custody before the magistrate; and all the newspapers full of the forgeries. In his rage, he took to venting execrations against his late employer.

"I hate him!" he screamed passionately, again and again, like a furious child. "I hate him! I hate him! I wish he were dead! I wish he were dead! Why didn't the roof fall in and crush him? Why didn't his cab break down and kill him? Why didn't the horse kick his brains out upon the roadway? Why doesn't some one take a knife and stab him? Such things happen every day. Why not to him? I hate him—hate him! I wish he were dead, dead, dead, a hundred times!"

Exhausted, he leant over the table, again hiding his face with his hands. For some time he remained silent, breathing hard. Then he started up with a cry. He felt himself touched on the

Noel Tredgold stood beside him.

"*You* here! at this time, of all others!" cried the old clerk, pressing his hands upon his forehead.

"Yes," Noel answered. "Do you wonder at seeing me? I have not been able to come before; though I have tried hard. I think John suspected me. He never let me out of his sight. But I have escaped him at last."

"What do you want with me?" William Moyle asked, peevishly.

"You told me my mother still lived. Where? Let me go to her."

There was something not quite natural about the tone of the young man's voice. He spoke with a sort of studied quietude and forced distinctness of articulation which was new to him. His apparent calmness of demeanour was probably costing him no slight effort. But the passion stirring deep within him was kept from manifesting itself outwardly; except that he was very pale; a steady but a fierce light gleamed in his eyes; and his hands were tightly clenched together—so tightly that the blood was driven from his finger-ends, and his nails were biting into his flesh.

William Moyle waited a few moments, trying to recollect. He had but a hazy memory of the scene in the studio in front of the medallion-portrait, and the revelation he had there made. He asked himself, with a puzzled look, What did Noel know of his mother? Finally, he abandoned all endeavour to settle the question, for an idea seemed to strike him. He started, and his face was lit up with a bitter, malignant, cunning look, which had something of savage joy about it.

"Come, then," he said.

And they went out.

Soon they were in a cab, hurrying along the high-road from London on the Middlesex side of the river leading westward. Did Noel remember the road? He had travelled it before. The last time was when he fled from Dr. Rawson's Academy to join Bryan Tredgold in the studio in Quebec Street. He took little heed, however, of the way they were speeding, of the incidents of the journey. He leant back in the cab, silent, frowning, with closely-locked lips. William Moyle was more excited, apparently; talked noisily of many things, and oftentimes stopped the cab to obtain refreshment for himself and the driver.

Some miles along the high-road, London a grimy cloud in their rear, and then they turned sharply to the right, down a narrow cross-road pleasantly shaded with beech trees, now strewing their leaves in a thick, tawny-hued carpet upon the way. Twenty minutes along this cross-road, and they entered a private carriage-drive between tall screens of dark shrubs and thick trees, with huge boughs stretched overhead, making in places quite a tunnel of foliage. They arrived in front of a large square stuccoed house, with a classical portico. This was "The Laurels," Mr. Gurwood's private asylum.

They were ushered into the library. The room was little changed since the reader saw it on the occasion of Mr. Gifford's visit, years ago now. Still over the fireplace was the long line of casts, the skulls of eccentric and deficient conformation—all so bald, with such closely-shut eyes, such harshly-lined lips, some depressed grimly at the ends, others fixed in a desperate grin or a mocking simper. Noel contemplated them sadly. Even at such a time, with other so different thoughts to engross him, he could not but reflect how different was this row of casts to the more familiar collection in the studio in Quebec Street. It was not only that the casts before him were taken after death; they were the heads of the insane. He had hardly appreciated as yet the character of the establishment to which William Moyle had brought him. And now the question came to him, thrilling, terrifying him, Was he to find his mother at last with a look upon her face—a dreadful look!—such as those faces wore? Could he bear to see her so? He grew faint, and clutched a chair for support.

The door opened, and Mr. Gurwood entered, bowing with an air of grave ceremony.

He had grown very fat. His face was larger and fleshier than ever, looking the more so from the fact of his hair having retreated from his forehead. His complexion was very sallow; but his eyes were not less bright than formerly under his heavy beetling brows, and he had the old strong decided look about his large jaws and protruding under-lip. He still kept his thick white fingers wide apart, as though they were sticky, raising them every now and then, when he mentioned the nature of the disease he made the specialty of his practice, to touch his forehead lightly, as though he were striking an octave of pianoforte notes. He contemplated his visitors calmly and thoughtfully. With William Moyle it was evident that he already possessed some acquaintance. They went apart, and held together a whispered conversation.

"It was not necessary, not at all necessary, to give notice of your visit," Mr. Gurwood said aloud. "I am quite ready to receive the friends of my patients at any hour they may do me the honour of visiting me. Pray sit down."

He pointed to seats, and sank into a large cushioned chair in front of a writing-table piled with books and papers.

"It is painful to me to have to state, that in the case of the patient in whom you are interested I am unable to report any successful issue to my long labours in a curative direction. Indeed I may say simply, that the instance presented by our patient is one of the most distressing, indeed *the* most distressing, I ever met with in the whole course of my professional experience—not a slight one; I may say, without presumption, not by any means a slight one. If we, who are charged with the care of sufferers under mental aberration, were ever to be induced to despond—but we never are—it would be in relation to such a case as that of our patient up-stairs."

He referred to one of the volumes before him, which appeared to be in manuscript, and to be arranged like a dictionary, with a list of cases in alphabetical order. He read, through gold-rimmed glasses, the heads of a long report, as it seemed.

"Dear me, how time runs on! I had no

idea that this was so old a case—really a very old case. But we occasionally find among the demented an extraordinary tenacity of life; really as though the body fed and thrived, if I may so say, upon the wreck of the mind. Dear me, the number of years this case has been under my charge! Here it is all at full length. 'ANN REEVE.'

Noel repeated the name aloud, with a startled cry.

"That is the name," Mr. Gurwood went on calmly. "Then we have the date of her coming under my charge; 'aged twenty-two; height, five feet three inches, about; fair complexion; sanguine temperament;' 'extreme debility;' 'pulse very irregular;' 'exciting cause of mental aberration, domestic affliction,' arising from circumstances not given; course of treatment pursued set out at great length, with the dates, medicines administered, etc., with full particulars —'acute dementia,' 'acetate of morphia, with warm baths,' and so on. Then we come to 'suicidal monomania,' and so on, a long story; until we arrive at 'settled melancholia.' Dear me, dear me! a very bad case; no intervals of reason that could properly be so called; 'general health very bad;' 'extreme prostration of bodily strength,' and now at last 'paralysis of the nether limbs.'" He closed the book. "Certainly a distressing case; if I were ever inclined to despond, as I said, it would be in relation to such a case as this. But the vicissitudes of insanity are very remarkable, very remarkable indeed. There is no predicting results in these cases. Still, I think I am almost justified in stating, that I cannot hold out any strong hopes of permanent amendment; no, not of permanent amendment. Would you like to proceed upstairs now?"

He led the way out of the room. Noel followed, moving like one in a dream. At the door he felt his arm grasped by William Moyle.

"Keep up," the old man said simply; and he did not release his hold, for he found that Noel had need of support—he was half fainting.

They followed Mr. Gurwood, mounting to the second-floor, and entered a small darkened room. A woman in spectacles, in a white cap, was sitting in the window mending stockings. She rose as they entered, and came forward.

"Well, nurse," said Mr. Gurwood blandly, cheerfully, "how are we going on to-day? What can you tell us about our patient?"

"Weary work, sir; weary work," said the

woman, looking over her spectacles, as she rose and put down her work; "never a word, nor a look, nor a movement."

Mr. Gurwood turned to his companions with an air that seemed to say: "There, you see, is it not as I told you—as I read from the copious notes in my case-book?"

As they grew more accustomed to the subdued light of the room, they could perceive a reclining figure in the small, neat, iron bedstead in the corner the farthest from the window; a figure of a woman apparently asleep, for she was quite motionless, with her thin, terribly thin, ivory-looking hands stretched out before her on the coverlet. Her eyes were closed; the faded face, with no vestige of colour left in it, was very wan and livid, with a strange unnatural look of age upon it; hollowed at the temples and the cheeks; the lips quite blanched. The hair had been cut short, apparently; a scanty lock or two of ashen-grey had strayed from beneath the neat close cap that she wore.

"No change from day to day?" Mr. Gurwood asked.

"No change indeed, sir," the nurse answered; "weary, weary work," she said again.

"As I stated,"—and Mr. Gurwood turned

again to his companions—" one of the most painful cases that has ever come under my notice. I have adopted every known form of curative treatment; I grieve to say, without any result that I can consider wholly satisfactory. Still, if even science fails us, we have time and patience and care to look to; and these will do much, very much; though I freely confess I should be sorry to hold out hopes that may only prove fallacious."

Noel had advanced to the bedside; he gazed on the worn lineaments, the waxen white face, so sunken, and haggard, and livid, it was pitiful to look on. He bowed his head reverently. Then, very tenderly, his fingers closed round the thin ivory hand upon the coverlet. A faint cry escaped him.

"What is the matter, my dear sir?" asked Mr. Gurwood; and he joined Noel at the bedside.

The woman's hand was deathly cold.

"This is very extraordinary, most extraordinary." With professional swiftness the doctor's fingers were at once on the wrist of the woman, then moved to her heart. A look of surprise and alarm appeared upon his face.

"Dear me, I had no idea of this! How is this, Mrs. Thomson?" he cried to the nurse.

"My poor mother!" cried Noel, falling upon his knees, "my poor mother! that I should see her thus!"

"What is it?" William Moyle asked eagerly.

"She is dead! She is dead!"

It was true. Death had determined the curative labours of Mr. Gurwood of "The Laurels," so far as this case was concerned. The patient—Ann Reeve, according to the case-book—was no more; had been dead, apparently, some hours; had drifted into death, silently, peacefully, painlessly, while the nurse worked at the window. Only one more note to be added to Mr. Gurwood's report now. "Dead; such a date."

"Not a hopeful case from the first," said Mr. Gurwood. "I expressly guarded myself from ever saying that it was. But everything possible was done for the patient. Be sure of that. It's a consolation to remember that now."

"*And this was the work of Richard Gifford,*" William Moyle hissed into the ear of Noel Tredgold; and then waited, as though to let the words sink deep and take root in the young man's heart. Noel did not answer; made no sign; it was as though he had not heard.

They were hurrying back to town again; the cabman lashing his steaming horse, eager to get from among the green fields and trees, back again to the streets and houses of town; lashing him perhaps unnecessarily; driving, indeed, rather unsteadily.

"Noel," William Moyle went on, "I saw your father, Bryan Tredgold, the first thing when he came back from Australia, from transportation. Would you like to hear what he said to me? I remember the words well. They frightened me, they were so fiercely spoken. For Bryan meant what he said. 'Moyle,' he said, 'if ever I prayed at all, I prayed I might come home to have my fingers, for five minutes, at Richard Gifford's throat! five minutes,' he cried, and he beat upon the table with his fist; I can see him do it now; I seem to hear his voice; 'half a minute would be enough.' His eyes shone so brightly, you'd have thought they were flashing fire. The two men never met; it would have gone hard with Richard Gifford if they had. Poor Bryan died before he could make his words good; before he could be even with that villain. And listen; a word in your ear. Bryan never knew what we know; he had no notion of Gurwood's patient; he thought her dead—your mother, Noel—dead of decline; letters were written to tell him so years and years ago. If he had seen what we have seen to-day—*all Richard Gifford's doing,* mind you, Noel, don't forget that—if he had seen what we have, I wouldn't have given much for Richard Gifford's chance of life! Bryan wouldn't have taken his hand from his throat till the man was dead, quite dead. And he'd have served him right—served him right. Bryan was a brave, strong man; he'd have killed that man as he would a wild beast; and he'd have done well! Oh, if he'd but have known of Gurwood's patient, not all the world would have held him back from Richard Gifford's throat!"

Still Noel made no answer. The cab whirled on, stopping only now and then at public-houses for drink for William Moyle and the driver, who both had had quite enough—more than enough. In their speed they failed to notice an old man journeying from town, who looked at them curiously, stopping to turn round and look, long after they had passed.

"What mad game is William playing?" asked John Moyle, for it was he. There was an expression of alarm upon his face as he cried, "Good Heavens! can it be? the scoundrel has been taking Noel to "The Laurels!'"

He was proceeding there himself, bent on one of those pilgrimages he was in the habit of making at stated times, journeying on foot, as though to a shrine, by way of penance, self-imposed for some wrong-doing in the past.

At "The Laurels" he was duly informed of all that had happened.

"Poor soul!" he said, as he stood by the body of Dr. Gurwood's patient; "her trials are over for ever." Presently he added, "If she could but have seen and known her boy!"—the tears coursed down his cheeks—"her poor boy Noel!"

Returning to town very late, he muffled up the medallion portrait in a cloud of crape.

Then he inquired for Noel. But Noel had not returned to Quebec Street; had not been seen since quite early in the morning.

CHAPTER VIII.

MR. GIFFORD EXPLAINS.

RATHER late in the evening, three men arrived in London after a long railway journey from the north-west of England. There was about all three a sunburnt look, a carelessness and rudeness of dress, which contrasted with the pallor of complexion and smugness of attire ordinarily characterizing Londoners. They talked very loud, after the manner of visitors from the country; took up a great deal of room on the pavement as they walked; were several times in imminent danger of being run over; and thought nothing of stopping suddenly in a straggling group that effectually incommoded the progress of the other passengers in the streets—also after the manner of visitors from the country. They walked to stretch their legs, as they said, having endured confinement for many hours in the train; and sometimes, with one accord, would begin stamping violently—as though they were rehearsing part of a new fancy dance they were importing for the entertainment of townsmen—to promote circulation in their lower limbs; for they had "gone to sleep" all over in the railway, suffering excruciatingly from "pins and needles"—especially in the feet.

"How this London's changed since I've been here! What a great overgrown beast of a place it is! A walk will do us good. We must take care we don't lose our way, though. But I should like, if I could, to set eyes on the laddie before I turn in. Then we'll have a hot tumbler all round, and get to bed. Hi! my man, is this the way to Quebec Street?"

Mr. Cluny Puckle was the speaker. His engagement with the Middle Wales Railway Company was at an end. He had been offered, and had accepted, an eligible appointment upon a railway in course of construction in the Island of Sardinia. He was in town to prepare for his departure, and to bid adieu to his old friend "the laddie," as he still persisted in calling Noel Tredgold. He was accompanied by Curate Griff and Williams the doctor, both in town for a few days' holiday with return-tickets.

They found in due time their way to Quebec Street, and received a kindly greeting from John

Moyle. They all agreed that the old man was much changed, however; his manner was so strange and excited.

"I always thought there was something of a bee in his bonnet," Mr. Puckle confessed. "It comes, maybe, of so much carving and graving of images all his life long."

But John Moyle could give them no information; indeed, seemed himself to be in a state of some anxiety concerning Noel. He thought it possible, however, that they might learn more of him by inquiring at William Moyle's in Whitfield Street.

"We'll go, then," said Mr. Puckle, who, by reason of his supposed superior acquaintance with town, assumed the chieftainship of the party. "I've been setting my heart upon a sight of the laddie before going to bed, and talking with him over a tumbler. How surprised he'll be at seeing us!"

But in Whitfield Street they found only Nance, desperately alarmed at the idea of three men calling at such a time. She answered their inquiries from the area. Her master was not at home; hadn't been since the morning. And of Noel Tredgold she had no knowledge whatever.

So the three men, rather gloomy and disappointed, were constrained to abandon all thought of seeing "the laddie" that night. They returned to their hotel. Mr. Puckle was inclined to be very angry with the waiter for bringing him Irish whisky instead of Scotch. But he forgave him ultimately.

"The poor creature," he said, "must get nearly daft with seeing so many strange faces every day; he can't be expected to discover what country they come from, or what drinks they'll like best, from merely looking at them. Ah, Griff, what are you doing? Putting more water in, when I've mixed it so nicely for you? Too strong? Not a bit of it. Look at the doctor. He's showing you the way. And he's going to have another glass, and so am I. And what do you think of London, Griff?"

"The noise of it, Cluny! I can think of nothing but that at present. And Noel! I wish we'd seen him."

"Here's the laddie's health. Nay, take the ladle out of the glass and empty it, Griff, like a man. One would think you were an old grandam sipping her tea."

To follow Noel.

Returning to town, he leant back in the cab,

silent and motionless; stupefied, as it seemed, by the terrible occurrence at Mr. Gurwood's asylum, by the discovery of his mother only in time to look upon her lifeless body. His companion was wildly garrulous, noisy, and incoherent. At first Noel paid no heed to him; but the ceaseless jangle of William Moyle's talk, enlivened now and then by meaningless laughter and tipsy screams, began in time to jar upon the young man's ear—to weary, to wound him. He felt grow upon him more and more a longing to be alone; to be left to his own thoughts; to be without a witness of his deep sorrow. He began to shrink from the sound of his associate's voice; to be acutely pained by it, as a wounded man flinches from touch—pales and quivers even at the mere apprehension of it. An extreme nervous sensitiveness came over him. If he had a task of vengeance to perform, as William Moyle again and again assured him, he did not need the stimulus of constant reminding. And at present, indeed, no violently wrathful passions were agitating him. He was possessed wholly by an agony of grief: in this every other feeling was for the time, at least, altogether merged. To be alone, to give the reins fully to his sorrow—this was all he asked. But this must be his at all costs. He availed himself of the first opportunity, therefore, to escape from a companionship that had become odious and unbearable; and on foot and alone he proceeded on the remainder of his journey back to town.

He saw with fervent thankfulness the cab pass on its way without him. He failed to notice, however, that the vehicle was most recklessly driven; that it was swaying about from side to side of the road; that the driver was losing control over his horse; was in a state of intoxication, hardly knowing where he was going or what he was doing. But Noel seemed to have no time to observe this, though others did, turning round as the cab went by to gaze after it, with a look of half-amusement, half-fear. Would the two drunken men in the cab reach town in safety? people asked. And why didn't the police interfere? It was shameful; it was dangerous. If there was really a special Providence watching over the inebriated, many agreed its protection was especially needed that day in the case of William Moyle and his cabman on their journey home from "The Laurels."

But Noel had not appreciated the fact that in quitting his companion he had escaped a position of some peril. He had been moved solely by the desire to be alone. He walked on slowly, seeing no one, heeding nothing. He might have been a somnambulist passing along the highway, he was so mindless of all external events. But for a time mental torpor always seems to succeed a state of violent emotion; numbness follows acute suffering, as though excess of pain in some way defeated itself: the victim writhes in agony under the first stripes of his punishment; but these in fact dull and deaden the senses to the blows that are to follow. This sort of drugged callousness, this semblance of indifference, however, is dearly purchased—brings with it special torments of its own. Utter dejection and hopelessness; the abandonment of every aspiration that can give value to life; the flinging away of all self-respect or care for self; of all right-thinking; of every barrier severing good from evil; the down-trampling of love, of purity, of religion; of every good and holy thing which humanity, in manifestation of its divine origin, has set store and price on, and raised altars to, and reverenced and worshipped—are these nothing? The terrible apathy that is born of exceeding misery! My poor Noel, rouse yourself at all costs from this. Shrink back from it shuddering; for it points ceaselessly to despair, and death—the death of the suicide.

Already the poor wretch was asking himself, why should he live? What was life worth to him now? Were it not better, better a thousand times, to lie in the Welsh churchyard by the side of poor mangled Bryan, his father, killed upon the works of the Mid-Wales Railway? or to go down into the grave with that poor dead mother, upon whose living face he had never looked, whose love he had never known, of whose very existence, prisoned in Mr. Gurwood's private asylum, he had never even dreamed? What was he to live for? How pitiful seemed every tie that could bind him to this earth? His art? He laughed mockingly at the thought. In his present mood he would have torn down with his hands, pounded beneath his feet, the noblest achievement art had ever wrought and perfected since it had been present among men. His love? It seemed to have died out of his bosom with every other noble and tender thought. His heart was turning to stone. Weep, Noel, weep; and bring it back again to softer stuff. No, not a tear! Can young eyes be so cold and hard and cruel? Pray, Noel; pray that into your heart may be poured the soothing and softening influence of that most excellent gift of charity, the very bond of peace and of all virtues, without which whosoever liveth is counted dead before Heaven. But his knees will not bend: he is rebelling against God. Alas! men have indeed need of an Omnipotent Father of infinite goodness and mercy.

If at this time he thought of Clare at all, it was only to assure himself again and again that she did not love him; that she had never loved him; that she had given him up without an effort, without compunction, at the bidding of —Richard Gifford. For that man she could find love and tenderness and submission: but not for Noel. She had chosen between them; let her abide by her choice. Yes; it was true, she could love this Richard Gifford.

His blood burned and tingled in his veins as he pronounced that man's name. It seemed to give some point and purpose and order to the throng of thoughts that were overwhelming him in a bewildering turmoil. He must find out this Richard Gifford. He had heard of him before, as William Moyle's employer; as Clare's step-father; as the head of the firm of Fordyce and Fordyce, somewhere in the City. He would see this man. It was he who had brought about all this terrible suffering and misery. It was all plain enough now. This was the man of whom Bryan in his final agonies had spoken, though he had concealed his name. This was the enemy whom poor Bryan had deemed a friend; who had charged him with a crime he had never committed; who had sustained that charge by a web of treachery and falsehood; had doomed him to a felon's fate, to a long term of prisonment in a penal settlement; who had done more than this —more than even Bryan, when he prayed to have his fingers but for five minutes at Richard Gifford's throat, had ever dreamt of. The poor soul secluded at "The Laurels" for long years and years! Why? And the fact hidden so sedulously from Bryan! Why was she called Ann Reeve? Was she not Bryan's wife? And with a crimson face Noel asked himself, Could it be that the Church had never hallowed the loves of his father and mother? Was he base-born? No, no; he would not think it. He would not so insult the memory of his father. Bryan—the good, the noble, the tender, the true, would he wrong so cruelly the woman he loved? would he bring shame upon her and upon her child? It was not possible.

Yes; he must stand face to face with this Richard Gifford. For vengeance? As yet he knew not, did not ask himself. Only he must see him. Afterwards, let come what come would.

But there was menace in his burning eyes, in his loudly-beating heart, in his clenched hands. It were well for Richard Gifford not to cross Noel Tredgold's path that night. Noel swore he would not close his eyes in sleep until he had confronted this man, who had wrought such terrible evil; until he had charged him with his wrong-doing, and bidden him render an account of his conduct.

There was night clouding the great city when Noel Tredgold reached its streets again. But a double line of gas-lamps garlanded Piccadilly; the shops glared with light, and the stars were spangling the skies. He passed along with a nervous, guilty feeling he felt it difficult to account for. He shrunk, not knowing why, from meeting the eyes of his fellow-men. He knew few people in London; yet he was possessed with a strange dread of encountering, in his present mood, any person who could claim acquaintance with him. It seemed to him as though he were engaged upon some secret mission of great importance, the objects of which he knew but vaguely, only that he must be let alone, left to himself, unrecognized, undiscovered. He was glad at last when the shops closed, when the throngs in the streets thinned. He counted these as so much more in favour of his design, though what that was he had no distinct idea. He would not go near John Moyle's house, that he knew; yet, with a start of alarm, he found he had been unconsciously and mechanically approaching the neighbourhood of Quebec Street. For no amount of money, he said to himself, would he meet John Moyle that night. He could not explain the feeling which led to this determination; yet he seemed to understand that John Moyle would hinder him in some way; but from doing what? He could not say. How he shrunk quite close to the wall when three men, walking together, passed him, touching him almost, whose voices he heard and knew, whose faces he saw and recognized! Three good, kind, trusty friends, who had travelled miles and miles to shake him again by the hand—travellers from the country, who, wearied with their journey, and strange to town, were yet taking pains to find him out, and interchange kindly greetings with him ere they went to bed. It was shameful, it was cruel, it was base; he let them go by, breathing more freely when they had passed. But he could not meet them now: he did not want to speak a word, or eat, or drink, or sleep, until he had stood face to face with Richard Gifford.

The office was in the City, he knew. He would go on there at once. After some search he found it, a policeman aiding him; but it was, of course, closed for the night. All the windows were dark; there was not a light burning in the house. He found a grim sort of satisfaction, however, in reading among the catalogue of names on the door-post the words FORDYCE AND FORDYCE; and then passed on, threading the labyrinth of narrow courts and streets environing the Bank of England—by day resounding with the clatter of thousand upon thousand of footsteps, with the hum of so many voices, the *sostenuto* accompaniments to the onward march of commerce; by night deserted and silent as a country churchyard. For hours and hours he walked on, or sauntered rather; for there was plenty of time before him. Round and round, never leaving the office of Fordyce and Fordyce far behind him, as though dreading lest it should disappear and be altogether lost to him if he did not keep near to it, with his eye constantly upon it. The police began to suspect him; could not understand his wandering about the City streets all the night through; and lay in wait for him, flattening themselves in shady doorways and dark corners, to emerge suddenly as he came by, and turn their lanterns well upon him, and take good note of him. But he did not wear a criminal look, his dress was respectable; he was pale and jaded and hungry-looking; but his manner was abstracted; he did not shrink from the lanterns, or turn away when the officer hove in sight; so that altogether, there were no sufficient grounds for his arrest and confinement in the station-house. One zealous constable certainly did go so far as to finger lightly and deftly the young man's coat-tails, expecting, perhaps, to hear the metallic clink of the cracksman's tools reward his enterprise. But he was disappointed. Noel did not carry a "jemmy," or crowbar, or a centre-bit. "Well, it's a rummy start, that's all," the policeman said to himself; "a lushy banker's clerk, with the key of the street, I suppose. But I don't know his face a bit. And he don't seem very lushy, either." Apparently satisfied, he troubled himself no further about Noel.

Round and round, up and down; a wearying business enough. Now he rests upon a door-step, till the chill breath of the night-air compels him to be up and walking again. Now wandering a little further, he finds himself leaning over a bridge, gazing at very early steamers, snorting and roaring and rousing themselves generally, getting up steam for a run to Hamburg or Rotterdam. Now, still further from the Bank of England, he is on a wharf, amidst the busy doings of a great fish-market. Here all are too occupied to notice his pale, young face, with its fixed, gaunt look, his strange, absent manner. Once, upon the bridge, a ragged, haggard woman had watched him, with a curious air of interest and alarm; for she thought she read the word "suicide" upon his face. Perhaps the poor soul herself was haunted by that word; saw it written in flaring capitals, turn which way she would. She seemed more relieved when she observed him turn and hurry away; for he always walked quickly back after these pausings, as though he were going to an appointment, and found himself behind time; as though he were a sentry who had neglected his duty, and was in haste to be back again to his post before his absence was discovered.

Soon, by the grey morning light, he could read the clock-face on the Exchange. Only a few more hours now to broad day: and these dragged slowly away at last. He did not move now from the door of the office. He could hardly yet expect Mr. Gifford, it was still so early: but presently an old housekeeper, with a ragged leather, was polishing the brass-plate; and now a figure was approaching, an hour or more before the time at which Mr. Gifford usually entered his office. Could this be he? Noel asked himself. Was this the man who had come down one afternoon in his carriage to Dr. Rawson's academy, and given a sovereign to the solitary schoolboy there, taking him abruptly by the chin? How old he looked; how changed, how broken! Still it was he.

"Mr. Gifford, I must speak to you."

"What do you want? You must come later; office-hours have not yet commenced. Who are you?"

He spoke querulously.

"My name is Noel Tredgold——"

"Come in," said Richard Gifford, with a start.

He led the way through his outer office to his private room.

"Sit down," he said, pointing to a chair; and he glanced at his visitor.

But Noel remained standing. Not so much in point of features, as in a certain expression and air and habit of attitude, he bore resemblance to his father Bryan. As he stood upright in Mr. Gifford's private office, this likeness was especially to be remarked. Perhaps Mr. Gifford thought so, and therefore turned away; certainly he could not keep his eyes on the young man; and his fingers wandered tremulously among the unopened letters upon his desk.

Earnestly as Noel had longed for this interview, prayed for it, waited through all the dreary hours of the night and morning for it, he had yet planned little what he should say to Richard Gifford on his first encountering him; or he had forgotten his plans. The passion to meet this man had been so great, that for the time it had submerged every consideration of what was to ensue upon that meeting. He was unstrung too, weak; wearied by his loss of sleep, his lack of food. He could not speak, his throat was so parched; his voice seemed to have died away.

Mr. Gifford, breathing quickly, the pulsation in his hollow cheek beating very fast, had left off fingering his letters. He was slowly opening and shutting a drawer in his writing-table, and touching now and then, moving it with a harsh sound upon the bottom of the drawer, a small, heavy, apparently metallic body; it might be a pistol. There was silence for a few minutes, while these two men were face to face.

"May I ask," Mr. Gifford began, in a low, faint voice, with ill-assumed calmness—"may I ask, Mr. Tredgold——" he stopped a moment, then said, "You prefer to be so called?"

"It is my name," Noel said abruptly.

Mr. Gifford bowed, smiled strangely, and continued—

"May I ask, Mr. Tredgold, the object of your visit?"

"Simply this——"

"Pardon me—before you begin—I am seriously an invalid; any excess of noise or excitement distresses me terribly. Pray speak in as moderate a tone as you can conveniently; and let me assure you, that I am not disposed for one moment to assume any position of hostility in regard to you. If I can render any assistance, can afford any explanation of circumstances that may seem to you strange in relation to your family history, so far as concerns my share in it, pray believe I shall be glad to be of service to you. I knew your father——"

"Bryan Tredgold? You admit you knew him?"

"Certainly. And I can trace in you a likeness to him, sufficient to satisfy me that you are his son. He was—you may be aware—a fellow-clerk of mine, in the employment of this house. Our acquaintance ceased, many years ago now, under very distressing circumstances. He was so unfortunate as to ——"

"Mr. Gifford," Noel broke in sternly, "I will speak of my father presently. But another matter first. I was yesterday at 'The Laurels,' a lunatic asylum, to see a patient of Mr. Gurwood's; a patient intrusted to his care by you. I arrived too late, however;" and his voice trembled, as he added, "when I reached the house, my mother had been dead some hours."

"She is dead?" Mr. Gifford cried, with real surprise. "Indeed, I was unaware of this. But I see before me a letter with a black edge; it is probably from Mr. Gurwood, announcing this sad occurrence. Poor creature! And yet, perhaps, it is wrong to regret her fate; for, as I judge, her state was utterly hopeless."

"In Mr. Gurwood's books his patient was described as ANN REEVE."

"That was so."

"Yet she was the wife of Bryan Tredgold?"

Noel spoke something at a venture—with no certain knowledge. Mr. Gifford paused. He was in some doubt, apparently, as to the extent of information possessed by his visitor.

"Yes," he said at length; "she was his wife."

Noel breathed more freely.

"If you ask," Mr. Gifford continued, speaking with much deliberation, as though carefully selecting his words, but quite as much watching their effect upon the person he addressed—"if you ask why her real—her married—name was not given, I answer, that it was concealed probably for the same reason that led your father to take an assumed name and hide his own. He called himself, I think, George Bryan, and was, by his own choice, so known for many years. Let us conclude that the motive for this suppression of the truth was sufficient in both cases."

Then there was silence. Mr. Gifford's calmness was less real than Noel imagined; still it irritated him, pained him he hardly knew why. He felt it was not for this cool, placid sort of discussion he had been at such pains to arrive at an interview with Richard Gifford. He grew angry with himself; he was dizzy and confused; he could not arrange his ideas; could marshal no array of charges against his opponent; could carry out no system of probing him by adroit questioning. And now to see a quiet, half-triumphant smile upon his foe's face, as if in enjoyment of his discomfiture! If his cause should fail from his bad handling of it! The thought was maddening.

"And this is the man proposed as a husband for Clare! This is Bryan's son! This Moyle's instrument of vengeance!" Mr. Gifford thought, contemptuously. "If I had known as much as I do now, I need not have been uneasy for a moment. He's but a poor creature!"

"Mr. Gifford," Noel began, in a pained voice, "I had many things to say—charges to bring, explanations to demand. Yet, I can't tell how, these things escape me at present. I am giddy and bewildered. Presently I shall be more myself, I dare say; but——" he stopped, then said abruptly, "The knowledge of his wife's existence was kept from Bryan. Why?"

"Ask yourself. Would the knowledge that she lived, hopelessly insane, an inmate of Dr. Gurwood's asylum; would this have rendered Bryan Tredgold happier in any way? Was it not better, a thousand times better, that he should think her dead, than to come home after his long exile to find her mad? Would it not have simply added to his suffering to know concerning her all that we know?"

Noel could not speak. The man was so

ready, so plausible, talked so deliberately; he was invincible.

"I think," Mr. Gifford went on, "you have been too ready to listen to those bent upon calumniating me. I can see the difficulty in which you are placed. Perhaps it had been better for *you* also never to have known what you do know. You were happier,—ask your own heart if I am not speaking truly—you were happier when you knew nothing of a very miserable past. A discharged servant of mine—discharged for faults patiently borne with for long years, yet growing on forbearance and kindness to a pitch that became at last absolutely unbearable—moved by a most venomous anger and a passion for revenge, has sought to stir up in you a violent feeling against me, and to turn to his own purposes your prejudices and animosities; to make use of you, in plain words, as an instrument for injuring me. You have credited only too implicitly all you have heard. It was perhaps pardonable. It is only natural a son should be eager to take upon himself the task of resenting wrong done, or what he conceives to be wrong done, to his parents. And you have been so wrought upon, that it is at last a disappointment to you to find that there is, in truth, no debt of vengeance owing between us.

Is this not so? I am prepared with ample explanations of every part of my conduct that you may deem it advisable to inquire into. Fairly, I might decline to hold all intercourse with you upon this subject; for, after all, what claim have you upon me? But I court investigation. I would serve you if you will let me; and I cannot serve you better than by exposing the man who would use you for his own dastardly ends. I would be your friend——"

"You were my father's enemy," Noel said simply.

"I was his friend as long as he let me be so. You distrust me still? Because I gave evidence on his trial; because it was in some measure through me that his conviction was secured. But what could I do? I was compelled to appear. I could not but state all I knew. I gave my evidence most reluctantly. It was not my fault that he was found guilty."

"He was innocent!" Noel cried.

"The court did not think so; the judge summed up against him; the jury were not five minutes in finding their verdict."

"And you?"

"I may have my own opinion on the subject. You still doubt?" He went to a drawer. "I have here an old newspaper containing a very full report of the trial, for the case made some stir. You will see the evidence in full of old Mr. Fordyce, the only representative of the firm at that time. The good old man could hardly speak for his emotion. There is the evidence of myself as chief clerk, of William Moyle, of the experts called in to speak to the erasures in the books, and such matters; but they broke down, I admit. Still you will see there was a very strong case against the prisoner."

Poor Noel held in his hands the soiled, faded newspaper containing the report of his father's trial. Tears—part of sorrow, part of rage—filled his eyes. He felt himself over-matched; Richard Gifford was winning an easy victory. No wonder. For a score of years he had been ready with his explanation. To do him justice, he was repeating it very glibly and cleverly, and it would have been satisfactory to everybody, perhaps, except the son of Bryan Tredgold.

"You can see for yourself that the case was a strong one. The large sums missing, the tampering with the books of the firm—the banker's pass-book among others—the erasures, and lastly, the finding in the prisoner's desk of money abstracted from the cash box, and expressly marked for the purpose of being identified."

"No more, no more; I'll hear no more!" cried Noel passionately. "On his death-bed Bryan avowed his innocence, declared he had been the victim of a cruel conspiracy."

"Did he charge anyone by name with conduct so base? No! Why, then do *you?* Why do you come to me with this charge? to *me* of all men? Did he once in your hearing make mention of my name? You confess he did not. Why, then, do *you* make an accusation *he* shrank throughout his life from making? And what motive had I, could I have, for wronging him so shamefully? He had married Ann Reeve, my cousin, my nearest living relation; against my wish I admit, but still the thing was done, could not be undone. Why should I plot to bring disgrace upon my own family? The money was gone; who had taken it? The frauds had been committed: by whom, if not by Bryan Tredgold? A breath of suspicion was never raised against another soul. *I* conspire to ruin him! Judge me by my conduct after his conviction. Who provided for his wife and the child that had then come into the world? Who, on his wife's reason abandoning her, secured her an asylum in the house of a medical man of great reputation—Dr. Gurwood's? maintained her there through a long course of years, up to her most sad ending yesterday? Who saw to the education of his son, placed him at school—a school highly recommended and well established—even though the boy might not have been happy there. There are matters here you may reflect upon, Mr. Noel Tredgold, with as much advantage to yourself and to others as the lying tales and infamous scandals to which you have been lately giving only too willing an ear."

And Mr. Gifford paused to pass his handkerchief across his forehead—he had grown warm and excited with talking—and to press his hand upon his left side. Presently he resumed:—

"For the concealment of names, for the mystery with which this affair has from the first been surrounded, it may have been right or wrong. But you will remember that on the spur of the moment, at a period of much distress and excitement, it is difficult to act with that calm judgment and discretion which a long lapse of years brings to the examination of a question. For my own part, I can truly say I did at the time what was judged by wiser heads than mine to be for the best. It was thought desirable to hush up as much as possible what was deemed to be a great scandal—to disconnect the wife and child from the disgrace incurred by the husband; to save my poor cousin from being pointed at as a felon's wife; to spare you the shame in after-life of being known, or of knowing yourself, to be a felon's son. Even now I cannot see that any great error in judgment was committed; and I am much mistaken if Bryan Tredgold himself did not acquiesce to the full in the views entertained by myself and others upon the subject. He concealed his real name even from you. Did he ever reveal to you that he was your father?"

"He did not."

"You did not make the discovery, you did not assume the name of Tredgold, until after his death?"

"I did not," Noel said, in a low voice.

Mr. Gifford smiled triumphantly. (There was some stir in the outer office just here; but the two men were so occupied, they did not heed it.)

"It seems, then, that the worst charge against me resolves itself into this: That by my advice information was conveyed to Bryan Tredgold, then a convict at Port Arthur, under sentence of transportation for a long term of years, that his wife was dead—had died of decline; whereas in truth she was alive, but insane. Possibly I did wrong; but at the time this poor woman, left absolutely to my charge as her nearest relative, was believed to be in a dying state. I had medical opinions that she could not possibly survive beyond a few days. The doctors were mistaken, but Bryan Tredgold was never undeceived. It was considered to be more merciful to him to conceal the fact of his wife's existence—regard being had for her most lamentable position—than to reveal it. If wrong was done by me under these circumstances, I am sorry; but, even from the worst point of view, I cannot think my conduct is open to very severe reprobation."

Mr. Gifford stopped; he had completed his explanation. He appeared to think that it ought to have satisfied Noel, and that his visitor might now take his departure. But as men cling to their faith with a mute persistence, which no amount of argument can affect in the remotest degree, which no subtlety of criticism can shake, because it proceeds from an innate conviction, a matter of internal feeling beyond the reach of reasoning, so Noel still hugged tight to his heart his firm belief that Bryan was innocent, that Richard Gifford was his foe. In this respect, all that could be said, however skilfully and cunningly, could work no change in him.

But he was deadly pale; his voice was strained and toneless, as he said—

"What you have told me, Mr. Gifford, may satisfy others; it can never satisfy me. I saw my father, Bryan Tredgold, on his death-bed. A little while before his death he spoke to me upon this subject, for the first and only time in his life. I, who knew him, know that he could never lie; that every word he spoke could only be the truth. He affirmed his innocence, and that he was the victim of a cruel conspiracy. You doubt me? Good God! I, who saw him die! His words are now sounding in my ears: 'I had an enemy, whom I, poor fool, deemed a friend, who plotted to destroy me; who brought this charge against me, sustained it by truth-seeming proofs, that were so many forgeries and lies. I did not think there was so much wickedness in man.' Not all the world could make me doubt the words my father spoke to me upon his death-bed."

Mr. Gifford winced a little at the young man's passionate cry.

"I have nothing more to say, unless I may be permitted to caution you against over-indulgence in a morbid feeling of sentiment. The explanation of my share in the misfortunes of your family is, I think, complete. I have no more to say. I have told you the simple truth——"

"Not all the truth," said a voice close to him.

The two men turned with a start of surprise.

John Moyle was standing in the doorway.

CHAPTER IX.

THE STORY OF THE PAST.

MUCH of the uneasiness and trepidation which had characterised Mr. Gifford's manner on his first encountering Noel Tredgold at the office-door had passed away in the course of their interview. He had recovered in great part his customary self-possession as the conversation proceeded, and he began to understand that the young man was likely to prove a less alarming antagonist than he had at one time conceived would be the case. Once or twice he had given evidence of some excitement of feeling; but this seemed to be roused rather by his own words—by a natural interest in the strength of his own arguments and explanatory statements—than by any apprehension that these would be unfavourably received by his visitor. It is possible that as, in the first instance, he was rather inclined to overrate the danger of the meeting, so, as time went on, he began to underrate it, and to entertain very depreciatory opinions touching Bryan Tredgold's son.

But the appearance of John Moyle effected a change.

Mr. Gifford paled, looked anxious; the pulsation in his hollow cheek beat quickly and strongly again. Once more he passed his silk handkerchief across his forehead, and pressed his hand upon his left side.

"Not all the truth," John Moyle repeated steadily.

Noel trembled with a new hope; he had been overcome, shamefully beaten; but, with this unexpected aid, might he not yet triumph? He knew nothing of what John Moyle had come to say; yet he would not, could not, doubt that this must be in Bryan's favour—must point to some weak place in Mr. Gifford's narrative.

"Why do you intrude here, Mr. Moyle?" Richard Gifford asked, with some fierceness.

"Not nearly all the truth," the old man said, not noticing the question.

"You will be careful what you say. You shall be held responsible for every word."

"Do not fear; I *will* be careful." And he bowed to Mr. Gifford. Then he turned to Noel. "My poor boy!" he said, tenderly; "there was fraud in the office of Messrs. Fordyce and Fordyce—forgery—embezzlement—call it by what law-name you will; but Bryan Tredgold had no hand in it."

Noel uttered a cry of joy.

"You dare say this?" Mr. Gifford demanded, with a gasp.

"I dare."

"The man is mad. He knows nothing of what he is talking. How should he? What *can* he know of this affair?"

"There was money missing — there was money taken; but not by Bryan Tredgold."

"By whom, then? Take care what you say, whom you accuse."

"Taken—alas, that I should have to say it! —by my own brother—by William Moyle."

The old man sighed sadly, bowing his head. Mr. Gifford laughed, not pleasantly, nor naturally.

"And you will get him to avow this—to accuse himself? A probable story, indeed!"

"Yes; he will do this."

"And he is prepared to take the consequences of his confession—to surrender himself to justice, if need be? Take care, I say," Mr. Gifford cried, with a threatening, cruel light in his eyes. "Where is your brother? Let him come here; produce him. Let him repeat this clumsy, lying story, this foolish attempt to take another man's guilt upon his own shoulders. Let him come and do this, here, now, if he dare. You have found him in some drunken fit, and given to his stupid blundering speech a false, mistaken meaning. Talk to him when he is sober, and he'll tell a different tale, I warrant." He spoke with an angry insolence, which had something wild and desperate about it. "There, we've had enough of this. You might have spared yourself the trouble of coming here to repeat a drunkard's babbling."

"Silence!" cried John Moyle, with some warmth. "Whatever have been William's faults, he is going where they will be judged mercifully. He, poor soul, has but a few hours to live. I was sent to see him very early this morning. He is lying in the accident-ward of the Middlesex Hospital. He was yesterday thrown violently from a cab, and the wheel passed over his body. Of his recovery there is no hope whatever. He is sinking fast; but he is quite sensible now. I have his permission to tell the truth concerning the past—the whole truth. He is going where your vengeance, your cruelty, cannot reach him,

Richard Gifford. He confesses freely that he was guilty of the crime for which Bryan Tredgold suffered punishment."

Noel advanced, and pressed the old man's hand.

Mr. Gifford turned deadly pale.

"Yet if this strange story should be true," he said, faintly, "what is it to me? How could I know of your brother's guilt? How could I judge otherwise of the charge against Bryan Tredgold than by the evidence adduced at his trial? He was judged guilty by the jury: how could I think otherwise than they did?"

"You *knew* that he was innocent; you *knew* who was really guilty. It was by you the frauds were discovered; and you discovered then also the person who had committed them. But you made it the price of my brother's escape that he should join you in a conspiracy to lay the guilt at Bryan Tredgold's door. The poor wretch consented—as he would, at such a time, have consented to anything that secured his own safety. More than this; at the time you appeared as a witness against Bryan Tredgold, you had in your possession a written confession, signed by the real thief; extorted from him as a sort of pledge of his fidelity, and part of the condition on which his own immunity was secured. That confession you have now. It has been an instrument in your hands to wield a cruel power over my wretched brother. Yes, and over me. It has compelled me to be silent until now; to acquiesce in oppression I shudder at; to connive at your most shameful schemes."

"You admit, then, you have had a share in the wrong done to Bryan Tredgold?" Mr. Gifford said feebly, with an attempt at a sneer.

"I do; and, Heaven knows, I have paid a price for my folly and my sin."

Mr. Gifford made an effort to rise; but he was weak and trembling. His voice sounded quite hollow, as he said—

"I am taken by surprise; but I have a complete answer to this charge; only"—he raised his shaking hands, and pressed them upon his forehead—"I am a little giddy just now; I am rather an invalid; and this excitement has been a little too much for me. Some other time I will see you again on this subject; and if you will listen to my explanations——"

He stopped; his lips moved as though he were still speaking, but no sound issued; his head sank upon his breast, and he fell heavily forward upon his desk. He had fainted.

His visitors summoned assistance, and left him.

From the lips of John Moyle the son of Bryan Tredgold learnt the story of the past.

There are many reasons however, why I should elect to set forth this other than in the old man's words. Not that John Moyle was an untrue or unfair historian, however; but for the thorough satisfying of the reader, particular points of the narrative require to be dwelt upon and elucidated; the motives influencing the several actors in the drama, including the sculptor himself, need to be investigated and accounted for; considerable annotatory matter has to be added; and it would be difficult for any one so closely concerned as was John Moyle in the events he was describing to accomplish this altogether effectively.

The story told to Noel Tredgold contained mention of an old naval officer retired to an out-of-the-way Cornish village, because living was cheap there, and he had need of all the money he could spare to educate his only son, and advance him in the world. George Tredgold, Lieutenant R.N. (he had never risen to higher rank: he had no interest, no "friends at court," and was not one of those men upon whom opportunities force themselves, as it were, and whose good luck enables them to dispense with such inestimable aids to fortune), had married, late in life, a Miss Bryan; he had given her surname by way of Christian name to his child; and had been left a widower after a very few years of wedded life. He was eager to grow rich—not for his own sake, but for his little Bryan's. He was a frank, simple, trustful gentleman, who deemed that his fellows were all as honest as himself. He was quite cut out to be a victim of the unscrupulous. He was induced to venture his entire savings in a bubble speculation—was ruined. His misfortune preyed terribly upon his health, upon his mind. He died by his own hand—leaving his son to the mercy of the world; the son of whom he had been so proud; for whom he had struggled so to save; pinching himself, denying himself the most trivial of luxuries—at sixty he had given up his pipe, thrown away his snuff-box, declined his customary glass of punch in the evening—to help make up a purse for Bryan, for whom he had planned a career so much more prosperous and happy than his own. Poor old man! his dreams were never to be realized. That cursed swindling mine! But at least he was spared something. In his moments of deepest depression—in those periods of insane gloom preceding his frightful suicide—he had never dreamt that his son would know the cruel sufferings which Bryan Tredgold was subsequently destined to experience.

To make a lad—a gentleman's son—self-supporting, there is but one way; hurry him up to London, and mount him on a stool in an office. He is soon in receipt of a small, but yearly increasing, salary. He can never, or very seldom, rise very high; he will probably be a drudge all his life; his career will be one of simple, dull, hard-working monotony. But at least he will not want bread; and he will probably not be unhappy, if his nature is unaspiring—if he is without ambition, without the restlessness, the longing for action, and change, and excitement, which distinguishes some men—marring many fortunes, making a few. Bryan Tredgold was taken from school; and exchanged the wild freedom, the healthy exhilaration, of his life on the Cornish coast, for long, long hours at a desk in the office of Messrs. Fordyce and Fordyce, in the City of London. How this piece of good fortune—for such it was under the circumstances, and considered soberly—was secured for him, matters little now. Failing an uncle or an aunt, thank God! there is always a kind clergyman or doctor, or other good friend, who will come forward to write letters, and take trouble, and be interested in, and give a helping hand to an orphan child.

The loss of his father, to whom he was tenderly attached, was severely felt by Bryan Tredgold. The change in his prospects that resulted was a much less serious matter to him. He was so young, that it was difficult for him to appreciate correctly the humble nature of the career he was now to enter upon as a junior clerk in Messrs. Fordyce's office. To a boy leaving school, any position that gives him, in however poor a way, an income of his own earning, seems an advantageous and desirable change, if only because it seems to bring him nearer to manhood. Youth is over hopeful, moreover; and the wearying sameness, the grinding routine, which were to be the characteristics of his future life, could not be at first apparent to him. He mounted his tall stool with alacrity, bent industriously over his books, eager in the first instance, at any rate, to serve his employers to the very best of his ability—though this mood did not last very long.

A strong, brave, sturdy-hearted, good-humoured fellow, with much of the frank cheeriness, the gallant carelessness, that had distinguished his father, the naval officer, in his young days, he was hardly the man to tie down to a life in a merchant's counting-house. The dashing soldier he would have made! the noble seaman! Carrying his life lightly in his hands, and hurling himself upon the foe, he should have been heard of fighting his country's battles wherever they were to be fought; or gaining the more peaceful laurels of successful arctic or tropical exploration and discovery; or restless whenever there was need of courage to endure and strength to act—a strong English arm, a stout English heart. Feebler nerves, weaker muscles, punier frames, could achieve as great things as he in the cramped arena of the merchant's office.

But he was too healthy, too manly, to repine. He made the best of his situation; his sturdy laugh could be heard now and then in the gloomy office, astounding by its strange loud music his fellow-clerks. They could not but be friendly to him. All were drawn towards him, as though there was some magical attraction for them in the very fact of his being so very different to themselves. They took pleasure in the cheery presence of the new-comer. Even the clerk who had been longest in the employment of the firm, who seemed to have so moulded himself to official manners and clerkly habits that he was less a man than an automaton; who was grey and bent, though then, in truth, as to years but in his prime; who was so quiet, so plodding, with an earnestness that had about it something stealthy and mysterious, even William Moyle—for so the clerk was named—even William Moyle was moved to welcome and show kindliness to the new-comer; inviting him to Lambeth, to the humble lodgings where he lived with his wife, childless—for as yet Liz Moyle was not born—proud of his gay, frank, handsome visitor; while Mrs. Moyle strove to do him honour, stirred herself to entertain him with appetising suppers, admired his bright eyes, his broad forehead, his thick mat of curly light-brown hair; both husband and wife recognizing and paying homage to the startling difference between themselves and their guest.

Bryan was very poor, of course; his income afforded him a bare subsistence. He was glad to get a roof over his head upon the cheapest terms possible. So, when he met at William Moyle's a relative of the family's, an older man, a sculptor in an humble way—John Moyle, in fact—and received from him an offer to rent, upon very moderate terms, a garret in Newman Street, where the artist occupied an upper floor, Bryan eagerly met the proposal. The room was very small, most scantily furnished, still it sufficed; and he was allowed, by way of sitting-room, free use of the sculptor's studio, was at liberty to come and go as he would. The poor are always kind to each other. Wanting money one's-self, the wants of others in the same respect are readily to be understood. It is the man with a full purse who has a difficulty in appreciating the feelings of his neighbour with empty pockets.

But perhaps John Moyle was not wholly moved by the necessities of his new acquaintance to show kindness to him. The sculptor was himself very poor, very obscure; found it hard to get a living by his art; was glad, indeed, oftentimes to put away his works in clay and marble, to busy himself less attractively with engraving seals for the stationers, or cameos for the jewellers; was compelled to be very saving; was falling into those habits of strict economy which he persisted in long after the need for them had disappeared, and which made a miser of him when fame and fortune were fairly his. He was glad to increase his own means even to the extent of the poor modicum of rent Bryan Tredgold paid to him for the garret in Newman Street. The young man was valuable to the artist as a lodger some time before he became dear to him as a friend. But this followed in due time. And at last a sincere attachment existed between the sculptor and the merchant's clerk. It was during their joint residence in Newman Street that accident brought in their way a lad from Scotland, wandering about London, very friendless and alone. They showed kindness to Cluny Puckle, he was in no hurry to forget. For a time room was found for him also in the house in Newman Street, and he became their intimate associate. At length he quitted them, having succeeded in obtaining an appointment, the object of his coming to town. He left England for India, to meet his former friends, long, long years afterwards, strangely enough, upon the works of the Mid-Wales Railway Company, under painful circumstances that have already been set forth.

Besides William Moyle, there was another clerk in the office of Messrs. Fordyce and Fordyce, with whom Bryan Tredgold established relations of some intimacy. This was Richard

Gifford, only a few years his senior, but a young man whose caution and cleverness and industry were already advancing him greatly in the estimation of his employers. On all sides, indeed, it was recognized that Richard Gifford was a man to succeed in his vocation. His manner was so staid and quiet, was so pervaded with a sense of self-respect; there was such an air of calm persistence about all he did; there was a feeling of power about him. He was handsome in person, with rather an unhealthy look, arising possibly from his unremitting attention to his official duties; he had a soft musical voice, and spoke in a deliberate, measured way. He dressed very simply, and had nothing of the frank gaiety and carelessness which might be looked for from one of his years. Indeed, there was very little of the young man about him; and he was constantly pointed out as an instance of that unusual condition of things, "an old head on young shoulders." The firm had implicit confidence in him; the firm being at this time represented by old Mr. Robert Fordyce, the only surviving partner, a widower with an only daughter, living in Berkeley Square.

But this faithful clerk, this industrious servant, was not so solely devoted to the interests of the house of Fordyce and Fordyce as at first sight he appeared to be; at least, he kept his own advantage constantly in view. A bright, eager light burned steadily sometimes in those dense black eyes of his. That quiet, composed manner, always deferential, yet never servile, masked no inconsiderable amount of ambition. He was thoroughly conscious of his own abilities—of the value of his services. He had taken exact measure of the chances in his favour. He was determined to rise in spite of all hindrances. He was persistently aspiring. Circumstances had compelled him to accept a humble position in the merchant's office. In the ordinary course of things, he was hardly likely to emerge from this. But he resolved that he would not be content with servitude all his life, however well remunerated and prized and appreciated. He would be master some day. He would keep that end steadily in view. By fair means or foul—for to himself he confessed that he had few scruples on the subject—he would have his will. Meanwhile—he showed no impatience—he could wait, working hard, watching ever, with thorough command over himself; never tiring, never throwing down his cards, or dreaming of so doing. Crafty, persevering, indefatigable, he became of more and more importance every day to his master. He never threw away a chance; there was no knowing but that the thing which seemed so remote might be yet in some way connected with his interests—might advantage him, might bring him nearer to his goal. He was everything to all men. He quarrelled with no one; he made friends where he could; was kindly and courtly ever; seemed to set a high value upon the good opinion of his fellows. Indeed, it appeared altogether that he was a man very likely to prosper in the path he had chosen.

Of course he never dreamt of making an enemy of Bryan Tredgold. Richard Gifford perhaps at first was rather inclined to despise the young fellow who had recently entered Messrs. Fordyce's office; who was so gay and careless, so harebrained; who had no ulterior views; who was without thought for to-morrow, provided to-day could be passed pleasantly; who, soon outgrowing his first impulsive industry, was not inclined to overwork himself; was not particularly desirous of the good opinions of his employers, if that could only be purchased by a toil and an assiduity which were hardly possible to him. But Gifford knew that this man could be no obstacle in the way of his plans. So he had no objection to Bryan Tredgold; was in time disposed to like him, indeed: was always friendly towards him in manner; was amused with his frank recklessness, his negligence, his candour, his want of ambition, his high animal spirits. The very contrast and difference that existed between the two men seemed to attach them to each other. Bryan respected while he marvelled at, and could not comprehend, his companion's conduct. He found a subject for admiration in the case of this young man, who was without the ordinary follies and indiscretions and imbecilities of young men in general; who toiled so earnestly at such distasteful occupations; who could interest himself with the dull routine of the counting-house; who was so staid in his habits; for whom there seemed not to exist in all London any pleasures or amusements "after office-hours;" who would take work home with him, though he received no extra pay for so doing; who was the first to come to the City, the last to leave; who sent no "sick-notes," never shammed ill, or took holidays. To Bryan there was something wonderful and unnatural in this. But he saw in it all only a man morbidly impressed with a sense of duty to his employers; and he rendered homage to a state of feeling he frankly avowed he could never experience himself. And between the two there existed, therefore, something which, if it was not friendship, was yet sufficiently like it to be accepted as such by a great number of people.

Years flew by without much change in the situation of either of the two clerks, except that Richard Gifford seemed to be more entirely in the confidence of Mr. Robert Fordyce; and, indeed, to have gained considerable influence over him. He was often a guest at the house in Berkeley Square, dining with his employer—an unusual honour for a clerk to the firm of Messrs. Fordyce and Fordyce, who had, as a rule, always held themselves much aloof in their private relations from their clerks and servants. But Mr. Robert Fordyce was growing old and infirm. He seemed to be the last male representative of his family. The question was already being asked, Who was to succeed him in the firm? And it was whispered in the office that Richard Gifford was aspiring to the hand of Miss Fordyce, and some amusement was drawn from the rumour. The lady was plain, with fiery red hair, and a bad temper—so it was said among the clerks. But unquestionably she would be very rich; and all agreed that it was quite worth Richard Gifford's while "to make up to her," if he thought her ugliness was outweighed by her wealth.

The passing years brought little change to Bryan, save that he grew bigger and stouter and cheerier, with more than ever of the heavy dragoon or the boatswain's mate about him, less than ever of the merchant's clerk; and some small additions had been made to his salary—not so much, perhaps, because of any increased deserving on his part, as that it was in the routine of Messrs. Fordyce's office to raise the rate of remuneration of their servants at stated periods. He was still popular among his fellows—the kind of man of whom people were fond of saying that he was "nobody's enemy but his own." Yet all agreed he was a good sort of man to have as a friend by your side, especially if you were in the midst of an unruly crowd, and a "row," or a "scrimmage" was likely to result from your situation. Few could stand up against Bryan's arm when he chose to let its full strength be put forth.

One change time did bring, however. He fell in love. He had a great tender heart, this indifferent clerk, this bulky, careless fellow. His love was no trifling matter. It grew out of his pity in the first instance; but it possessed him very absolutely in the end. He loved with all the strong thoroughness of his nature.

She was just the woman to be loved by a brave, sturdy man. She seemed to have so much need of his protection and compassion, of refuge in his strength and courage. A timid, shrinking girl, very beautiful, very slight and delicate, poor as himself, and left almost alone in the world—little able of herself to proceed along the trying paths of life. She was a daily governess. He had long been in the habit of meeting her as he journeyed every morning down Oxford Street and Holborn on his way to Messrs. Fordyce's office. He learnt to take a great interest in this pale, gentle lady passing punctually on her way to give lessons to her pupils. He pitied her timid air, her sweet young face. He worked himself into a rage every time he dwelt upon her cruel fate; he railed angrily against fortune when he met the poor governess out in the bitter weather, struggling with the wind, pelted by the rain. He longed to lift her in his arms—the task would have been an easy one enough—and carry her wheresoever she would, not permitting her feet to be soiled by contact with the wet pavement, with the miry road. Yet he could do nothing: to address her would have been an insult. She could be nothing to him, or he to her. He was cut to the heart at the sight of her sufferings, at the thought of his own powerlessness to be of use to her.

But opportunity befriended Bryan at last. A street Lothario ventured to test the power of his fascinations upon the governess, wholly unprotected as he thought. He was mistaken, and paid penalties. Something very hard met his face; sparks danced before his eyes; the whole world seemed turned for the moment of a scarlet hue. Then he was in the gutter bathed in mud, the blood was trickling prettily down his cheeks from a star-shaped wound above, his hat was under the wheel of an omnibus, his coat was split up the back, and two or three of his front teeth he could never find any more, let him try as hard as he might—perhaps he had swallowed them. Bryan could best have explained how all this had come to pass; he was certainly on the spot at the time. And afterwards he had made the acquaintance of the governess. He was the more timid of the two when they came to talking, however. Brave men are often bashful. But all difficulty on this account wore away in time. They could hardly help becoming friends. He went east daily, she west, at the same hour in the morning. It was inevitable that they should meet somewhere on the road.

The governess was Ann Reeve. She was engaged daily giving lessons in music and singing (so in time he learnt) to Emily, only daughter of Mr. Robert Fordyce, of Berkeley Square; and she taught other pupils in the neighbourhood of Hyde Park. She had lost both father and mother; her orphan state seemed to draw her nearer still to Bryan Tredgold. He looked upon her with the sort of pitying fondness with which a strong man contemplates a helpless child. He loved her very tenderly, longing for the time to come when he could take her to his arms, and shield her from the world; when she should cease to be exposed to the weather, should give no more lessons, should be his own—his wife. His poverty had never seemed so hard to bear as now. With his humble income, could he dare to marry? Meantime he could only offer her his love—very whole and true and earnest. For a time he kept this hidden in his heart, afraid to speak of it, lest he should scare her from him. But he revealed his secret at last—in broken words, breathlessly—with a thumping heart, and earnest, frightened eyes. She had loved him from the first. She made no other answer than to hide her tearful face, resting her head upon his breast. But the action was as eloquent and to the purpose as all the words in the world. How happy Bryan was!

This had happened in a quiet walk in Hyde Park. Bryan had stolen away early from the office to meet the governess returning from the west. They had turned out of the noisy highway for quiet converse in the Park. And there they talked for the first time of love. I don't know what the park-keeper must have thought of them. Perhaps he had loved himself, and had sympathy for an engaged couple, and looked another way. They were too much occupied with themselves to heed him. As they came away, Bryan looked handsomer than ever—from sheer happiness, which is very becoming, suits all complexions; and for Ann Reeve, there was a bright light in her eyes, and a colour in her cheeks, such as had never been seen there before. The love hidden in their hearts for some time now sparkled publicly on the surface, like gold fresh dug suddenly from an unsuspected mine.

The lady had another votary, of whose worship, however, she never knew. Farther on her way than the point at which she was accustomed to meet Bryan, she was often passed by a shabby, old-looking, homely man. This was John Moyle, sculptor, who, his companion gone to the City, took a morning stroll in Oxford Street before he commenced his daily labours. He hardly seemed to look at her as he shuffled past. Yet he, too, loved her, with a strange furtive sort of love, very earnest, very concentrated. It was the one romance of a toilsome, painful, struggling life. And for a time he seemed only to live for this all-absorbing yet hopeless passion of his. He breathed no word of his love, however; to adore at a distance was all he asked. He knew from the first that she could never be his, could never care for him; for he was without the vanity which in such cases always gives birth to hope. Yet when he knew that the object of his idolatry had given her love to Bryan Tredgold, he was near to hating his friend. He locked himself in his studio; for he felt his mind reeling, and was conscious, with the subtlety of insanity, that if he were at large, it would be to the detriment of his fellow-men. Above all, he shrunk from meeting Bryan; dared not encounter his glance; writhed with pain when he overheard by chance his friend's joyous tones, full of the music of triumphant love. How they jarred upon the sculptor's ear!

And by and by Bryan learnt from Ann, as a sort of secret, that she was related to Richard Gifford, Messrs. Fordyce's exemplary clerk and indefatigable servant—was, in fact, his cousin. But this was not so generally known, and was not to be talked about. Indeed, it was evident that the lady stood in some awe of her relative.

CHAPTER X.

BUSINESS IS SUSPENDED.

Partly, perhaps, from an unworthy pride, partly from its being in his nature to be reticent and reserved, partly from a vague fear lest disclosure should in some way affect his interests and interfere with his plans for rising in the world, Richard Gifford had kept the fact of his relationship to Ann Reeve, the governess, strictly concealed. Yet she was almost his only surviving relative; and he was in a measure charged with the protection and care of her. Possibly it was through his interest that she originally obtained her situation at Mr. Fordyce's in Berkeley Square; but certainly it was never suspected by Mr. Fordyce or his daughter that the governess was the cousin of the clever clerk in the City office.

Ann Reeve was afraid of her cousin. For in a confused, troubled sort of a way, he had more than once spoken of his love for her; and she had shrunk from him. His words awoke no echoes in her heart, stirred up no strange thrills of passion, fired no hidden train of exquisite emotions. She trembled beneath his gaze; but it was with cold or fear, not love. There was something harsh and repellant about his affection for her, as though it were involuntary, betraying itself in spite of him, struggling with and mastering him. Fierceness, anger, cruelty, were all strangely commingled in his love.

In truth, as there was much restless ambition, so also there was much agitation and suffering concealed beneath the calm, cold demeanour of the merchant's clerk. He really loved his cousin; had long loved her passionately; and the conflict between his affection and his self-interest was a bitter one. If he married the governess, his hopes of fortune and success were at an end for ever. Clogged with a poor wife, he was assured that his future rise in the world was no longer possible; he could be thenceforth but a clerk and a drudge all his life. He was not capable of such a sacrifice. Bryan, it might be from carelessness, but it was rather, I think, from the magnitude and integrity of his love, had never troubled himself with, could hardly, indeed, stoop to, such considerations. But Richard Gifford was made of different stuff; and he was for ever asking himself whether he might not marry, not the governess, but the pupil. As the husband of Emily Fordyce, fortune would be secured to him. He could contemplate with certainty, first a partnership with his father-in-law, ultimately the sole representation of the old firm of Fordyce and Fordyce. He began to bend all his energies to the accomplishment of this object. He surrendered himself to his ambition.

And yet, with a curious inconsistency, he would not abandon his love for his cousin; was furious at the thought of yielding her to another. He would not marry her himself, and yet he could not endure the idea of her being called "wife" by any other lips than his. It may be that, hardly confessed to himself, there yet lay hidden in the depths of his heart some unholy thought of his possessing Ann Reeve, but in a dishonourable and shameful way. If this idea existed, however, it had not shaped itself into any defined plan of action. Meanwhile, to do him justice, he avoided his cousin as much as possible, taking care to avail himself of every opportunity that drew him nearer to Mr. Fordyce and his daughter.

It was little likely, it was not in the nature of the man, that Bryan Tredgold should make much secret of his love. He never dreamt of the malignant hatred he would draw down upon himself by the avowal of the fact. But Richard Gifford could not forgive a success bought, as he conceived, by his own failure. He trembled with rage as he became compelled to acknowledge that in one respect, at least, Bryan was his superior—triumphed over him. For if in nothing else, Bryan was likely to prosper in his love—to win the heart of a woman. And he deserved to succeed, his love was so absolute, so wholly unselfish, so all-absorbing. About its very rashness and improvidence, its impetuosity, there was an irresistible charm. To a woman, her lover's very unreasonableness has an attraction far beyond the prudent forethought and judicious caution which distinguish calmer admirers; for in these last she is apt to detect more care of themselves than love for her. And Bryan was tenderly loved by Ann Reeve. Not all Richard Gifford's scoldings and threats—and he did not spare them—could turn her heart from her lover. She wept: it was not difficult to bring tears into those soft brown eyes; she covered her face; she implored her cousin to be silent, to spare her the acute suffering his words occasioned her. But she remained true to Bryan.

Gifford was not a man to stop at hating; he

swore he would make his hatred felt, he would crush his enemy—for so now he accounted Bryan Tredgold. He would end for ever this foolish love-affair of his cousin's; it should be nipped in the bud. Bryan Tredgold should never triumph in the possession of Ann Reeve.

After some time it became evident that there was something wrong in the accounts of Messrs. Fordyce and Fordyce; that an ingenious system of fraud was being carried on. Perhaps, if Bryan Tredgold had been moderately careful, had not taken things too much for granted, had checked additions and examined writings with a little more deliberation, he would have detected the malpractice long before—arrested the system at the outset. But at this time his attention was greatly diverted by his own affairs. And, indeed, he was entirely ignorant up to the moment of his arrest, even of the fact that there had been unlawful dealing with the property of the firm. Mr. Gifford devoted himself to the detection of the thief; and soon pounced upon William Moyle. The elder clerk, it appeared, had been engaged in much public-house betting upon horse-races, and had become involved to a considerable amount. He supplied himself from the funds of his employers. His defalcations were at first trivial, but became more serious as he grew bolder; time went on, he remained undiscovered, and his necessities increased. Upon detection, the compact described by John Moyle followed. Gifford's first idea had been to implicate Bryan also in the charge of fraud. And, indeed, the young man's confessed negligence gave some colour to the accusation. But, as further examination proceeded, Gifford found he could not hope to secure in this way the conviction of his enemy. He changed his plan, therefore. He was content to let William Moyle escape—more, to retain him in his situation as clerk; for that was inevitable: the theory of Tredgold's guilt could only be sustained by the theory of William Moyle's innocence. And it was part of the agreement between the two conspirators that Moyle should remain in the service of the firm, with earnest promises of amendment—fulfilled in the future, so far, at least, as his honesty, not his sobriety, was concerned. The ruin of Bryan was no longer difficult of achievement. And to assure his downfall, marked money was found in his desk by those who had placed it there for the express object of so discovering it, and who readily identified it as money taken from the cash-box of the firm. It was only at the last moment that Bryan had consented to the engagement of counsel on his behalf. Satisfied of his own innocence, he could not imagine that it would be less clear to the judge and jury than to himself. He was, as we know, found guilty, and sentenced to transportation for a long term of years. In those days transportation was more in vogue than at present. Colonies were less squeamish as to the character of their population; and failing more respectable emigrants, were glad to put up with convicts.

Instinctively Bryan knew at last who had been his foe: his former friend, the cousin of Ann Reeve—her angry and jealous, because disappointed, lover. He denounced Richard Gifford as the cause of his suffering. He acquitted all others; never suspected William Moyle's share in the plot, or, at most, looked upon him only as a helpless, unconscious instrument in the hands of the other conspirator. But against Richard Gifford his anger knew no bounds. Upon Richard Gifford he swore he would some day wreak a terrible vengeance.

Gifford triumphed. He had crushed his rival. Had he also crushed out the loves of Ann Reeve and Bryan Tredgold? His success was less complete than he had expected. Something had happened the possibility of which he had never taken into account. At the time of the trial it was discovered that Bryan and Ann had been some months secretly married.

For John Moyle's share in these events it may be stated, that he was from the first satisfied of Bryan's innocence. He constantly visited his friend during his confinement before the trial, cheering him with the hopes of complete acquittal and release. Of course the sculptor knew nothing of the plot to ruin the prisoner; nor indeed did the wife of William Moyle, who was also assiduous in her efforts to encourage Bryan, and to comfort, as far as was possible, his unhappy wife in his absence. But on the eve of the trial, William Moyle, touched it may be by the desperate confidence which was leading Bryan to refuse all extrinsic aids to his defence in reliance upon his own innocence, aware of the strength and completeness of the case which was to be brought into court, and anxious that all chances in his favour should not be lost to the accused, but that at least the best possible advocacy should be secured on his behalf, let fall, in the presence of his brother, John Moyle, some unmistakable hints as to the real state of the case. For a time the sculptor seemed quite unable to credit what he heard; was then paralyzed by shame and terror. Gradually the whole story was revealed to him in all its shameful minutiæ. He learnt too, that, as part of the price of his own escape, William Moyle had deposited a written confession of his guilt in the hands of Gifford; had so delivered himself, bound hand and foot, as it were, into the hands of his fellow-conspirator. What was to be done? Could John Moyle avail himself of information obtained under such distressing conditions? Could he ruin his brother to obtain Bryan's discharge? William Moyle was on his knees, imploring pity and secresy. He would not let his brother go until he had sworn solemnly never to betray the real culprit; to keep the cruel conspiracy, of which his friend was to be the victim, a secret for ever.

Pale, feeble, trembling, he yet stirred himself to do what he could for Bryan. Counsel was retained for the defence; but there was little time to study the case; the evidence was fearfully strong; the lawyer's efforts were altogether in vain.

Bitterly John Moyle, in after years, reproached himself for his share in Bryan's condemnation. There was something almost unnatural about the severity of his self-accusation, or there were more grounds for it than were immediately apparent. Was there any secret reason he could charge himself with, though others could not, for his lenity to his brother? for his silence when the sentence against Bryan Tredgold was spoken? This may have been so. John Moyle had, as we know, loved Ann Reeve. Had he permitted himself, however feebly or transitorily, any sense of satisfaction in the fall of the man who had won her? any wild wicked thought that, in Bryan's ruin and inevitable separation from his wife, the hopes of her elder unsuspected lover approached, but in ever so small a way, nearer to fulfilment? Who can answer these questions? It is hard to search thoroughly, or to judge fairly, the strange thoughts stored in the heart of a man.

In any case, poor Bryan never doubted him. Setting forth on his terrible exile, he bequeathed to him the care of his wife, and the child she was presently to bring into the world. John Moyle accepted the trust eagerly; and betrayed it. He was very poor at the time, and was moved in some degree, perhaps, by those miserly considerations which were then taking strong hold of him; but, still more, he was influenced by the uncompromising demands of Richard

Gifford, who seemed to have obtained complete control over the brothers; and at last he relinquished all claim to guardianship. The care of Bryan's wife and child was thus left absolutely to the last man he would have chosen for a trust so precious—to Richard Gifford!

But the shock of the trial and the sentence had been too much for Bryan's wife. Soon after the birth of her son,—the Noel Tredgold of this history,—her reason left her for ever. During the remainder of her life, strangely prolonged, all the sad circumstances of her case being considered, she was restrained in Mr. Gurwood's asylum. John Moyle journeyed there constantly to see her, as we know. His visits were dictated by his sense of duty to Bryan, or by his deep love for the suffering woman. Something, too, there may have been in the nature of a self-imposed penance and mortification about his pilgrimages to "The Laurels;" certainly they could only have occasioned him very acute pain.

Richard Gifford had placed his cousin under Mr. Gurwood's care in her maiden name of Ann Reeve, and refused to acknowledge her son but as Noel Reeve. His animosity against Bryan Tredgold seemed even to grow rather than to abate as time went on; there was something of the fury of impotent or baffled rage in his vindictive feeling against his victim. He took a pitiful pleasure in ignoring his cousin's marriage; tried not to think of her as his rival's wife; as though he could alter the truth, or overcome facts by simply denying them. He could not bear to hear the name of Tredgold; it made him blench and shiver. But the coward is always cruel and implacable; and Richard Gifford was in a great measure deficient in physical courage. In this, perhaps, his chief punishment consisted. He could not look forward but with nervous apprehension to the time when Bryan would be released, and at liberty to return to England. His dread of personal violence—for he conceived Bryan's threatened vengeance would assume that form—was for a long time excessive. He kept himself informed of the convict's movements; and when his return became imminent, conscious of his own inability to cope with Bryan in any hand-to-hand collision, he armed himself with pistols, entered into communication with the police, and prepared for the worst. It was indeed his morbid anxiety to prevent any further kindling of Bryan's wrath against him that induced him to conceal the real state of the case in regard to Ann Reeve, or Ann Tredgold, as she should rather be called. He was in a sort of panic at learning that her recovery was considered to be utterly hopeless. He felt that her insanity would be charged to his cruelty by Bryan, if by no one else, and that the debt of vengeance which the convict had sworn would be one day paid in full, would be thus terribly increased. He caused information, therefore, to be conveyed to Bryan that his wife had died of gradual decline. Her health had always been delicate; she had even manifested at one time a consumptive tendency, and her death from such a cause seemed a natural event enough, and, however grievous to Bryan, less likely than her insanity to be considered by him as a result of his enemy's relentless persecution. If, on his return, he had seen the woman he had loved so tenderly a patient, hopelessly insane, in Mr. Gurwood's asylum, and the thought had come to him, that in this also he beheld something more of his foe's evil doings, who can say to what acts of violence, in his rage and agony, he might have been driven? Fortunately he was spared this. He had seen Ann Reeve only in her youth and beauty; it was better so, a thousand times.

Still Richard Gifford had misjudged his victim; as an evil-minded man invariably fails in his appraisement of the good in his fellow-creatures, underrating it lamentably. He did not understand that Bryan Tredgold, cruelly injured and outraged as he had been, was yet a Christian. As we have seen, the convict came home, to abandon his dream of vengeance; to avoid his oppressor, shrinking even from the chance of meeting him, and the temptation that would thereby ensue; to labour humbly for his bread; to win the love of a son he loved too dearly to own and claim, lest he should divide with him the disgrace and sorrow of his life; came home to die a ganger upon the railway works. Poor Bryan! a sad fate; but better, God knows, than the fulfilment of the fondest dreams of retaliation.

Meanwhile the clever clerk had risen in the world. In due course he had married Miss Fordyce, Herbert Gifford being the only child born of that union. But he was still only a clerk in the house when his wife died. Not long afterwards, however, he benefited his position by a second marriage. He became the husband of Mrs. Gray, his present wife, the widow of the late Honourable Ferdinand Gray, and the mother of Clare. This advantageous match enabled him to become a partner in the firm of Fordyce and Fordyce, and, on the death of old Mr. Fordyce, to occupy the proud position of being its sole representative.

Much of this story, fuller in some particulars, scantier in others, John Moyle told to Noel Tredgold, listening with worn, eager face, white lips, and tearful eyes.

"My poor father!" he moaned; "my poor mother! How terribly they were tried! how cruelly they suffered!"

"Can you pardon me, Noel?" John Moyle asked. "Can you pardon me my share in their trials?"

Noel gently pressed the old man's hand. "You loved her!" he said, in a low voice.

John Moyle bowed his head. He was silent for some time. Presently he said—

"How Bryan bore his trials, you yourself know. Your mother, poor soul, sunk beneath them. And you, Noel, what will you do?"

The young man cried passionately—

"One thing at least I will do: I will compel this man, this monster, to proclaim aloud my father's innocence, and his own infamy."

Recovered from his fainting-fit, but still very weak and suffering, Mr. Gifford had remained in his office. But he had locked the door, and refused to see any one. All visitors were to be told that he was ill, or absent. Many people called to see him during the day; and there was some clamour in the outer office. He heard himself charged, noisily and insolently, with "keeping out of the way on purpose." It was evident, indeed, that things were going very badly with the old-established firm of Fordyce and Fordyce. But he took no heed; he did not stir. Yet he was doing nothing—leaning upon his desk, hiding his face in his hands. His carriage came at the appointed time, to carry him back to Cumberland Crescent; but he dismissed it. He could not yet leave the City, he said; he would return home at his own time, in a cab.

The daylight waned; and soon night was darkening the office. Yet he would have no candles lighted in his room; he still sat at his desk, leaning his head upon his hands, and hiding his face. The clerks, with wondering looks, conversing together in awful whispers, took their departure. The office was closed for the night. The City was emptying; the work of the day was over; Commerce was going to snatch a few hours of feverish rest, and awake to renewed toil on the morrow. Still Mr. Gifford sat alone in his dark private room.

The old housekeeper, coming in to sweep the office, started back with alarm at seeing him; she quite lost her breath.

"Don't be frightened," he said.

There was a curious hollowness about the tone of his voice.

"I beg your pardon, sir," the housekeeper gasped, curtseying; "I thought everybody had gone. I didn't know there was any one here. In the dark too! it quite startled me."

"I'm going directly. Leave your candle, and fetch me a tumbler of water."

She went to comply with his instructions. He took up a pen, and hurriedly, and not without difficulty, wrote a few lines upon a half-sheet of paper. She returned with the water. His hand shook, and the glass clicked against his teeth as he held it to his lips. He drained it, and set it down.

"You are not looking well, sir," the housekeeper said, timidly.

"I am not very well," he answered.

"You work too hard, sir, if I may say so. You ought to have a change, sir. You ought to consider your health, sir. You must take care of yourself indeed, sir."

"I shall be better soon," he said, faintly. And he stood for a moment with an uncertain air, waving the sheet of paper to and fro, as though to dry the ink. Apparently he had forgotten that he had already passed the blotting-paper over it.

"I don't think I shall be here to-morrow——" he began; and he stopped.

"That's right, sir; take a holiday."

He did not notice the housekeeper's remark.

"You will close the outer door of the office, and wafer this notice on the door." But he did not quit his hold of the paper.

"Very good, sir," said the housekeeper. "Shall I go out and get you a cab?"

"No, thank you; I'll walk. It's fine, I think; I shall be better for a walk. You will be particular about this paper; take care of it, and wafer it on the door the first thing in the morning."

"I'll be sure to, sir; you may rely upon me."

The paper was in her possession. Mr. Gifford lingered still, eyeing it curiously.

"You've been housekeeper to the firm many years?" he said, suddenly.

"Many a long year now, sir."

"There!"—he placed some money in her hand. "Good night!"

And he hurried out. His footsteps could be heard resounding along the narrow way. Then he was lost in the darkness, and all was silent.

"As like a ghost as he can look," said the housekeeper. "Poor gentleman! and he's given me ten sovereigns. What for, I wonder? A good and kind master, for all he seems so stern."

She turned to read the notice to be wafered up on the morrow.

It was as follows:—

FORDYCE AND FORDYCE.

Business is suspended, and the Office is closed pending negotiations.

All letters, etc., are to be left with the Housekeeper.

The date and the initials R. G. were added.

"Good heavens! what can it mean? Can Fordyce and Fordyce have broke? No; it's not possible."

CHAPTER XI.

A DEBT OF VENGEANCE.

There is always some risk of failure attendant upon a project which aims to give enjoyment to one's friends by taking them by surprise. Coming upon them suddenly after a prolonged separation, it is easy enough to succeed in startling, but we cannot be equally sure of conferring pleasure upon them. A safer plan is certainly to give timely warning and pre-arrange meetings, so that both parties to the treaty of friendship may come together, having had opportunity to subside into a fitting state of mind, and prepared to resume their understanding with each other upon the same terms of intimate friendliness upon which they parted. This is so busy a world; events come crowding on in such quick succession, that men imperceptibly, and without intention, undergo an inevitable process of change, induced by the new crop which each day brings forth of hopes and thoughts and plans to occupy and divert; and it is not, therefore, simply a question of time which has to be considered in the case of separation from our friends. Who has not felt the difficulty of taking up again precisely at the point at which it was quitted, a friendship which unavoidable circumstances have for a long time suspended? Who has failed to perceive that during the unfortunate interval, many ties that erst seemed substantial enough have completely worn away, others have become terribly unravelled, or tried to the uttermost by the strain put upon them, and that altogether there is very much work to be done over again? It is not a comfortable reflection, perhaps, that the love or the friendship which can withstand the trials of time and separation is exceedingly rare. We must carry the charge to the debit of our human frailty: although that side of the account is already heavy enough, in all conscience.

The meeting of Noel and his three friends, travellers from the north-west, was friendly enough; they interchanged cordial greetings; and yet on both sides was a feeling that verged in some way upon disappointment. Noel could not but be sensible that about the arrival of his old associates at such a moment there was something inopportune—all things considered—while on the other hand Mr. Puckle and his companions were conscious that their coming was to some extent a failure; had not conferred either upon themselves or the subject of their visit the gratification they had anticipated. The three excursionists agreed among themselves, grieving the while, that "the laddie" was rather constrained in manner, wore a pre-occupied, a suffering air, had lost his old, bright, frank, gladsome look; that, in short, there was something decidedly wrong about him.

"His hand was very feverish," Williams, the doctor, observed, "very feverish indeed. I noticed it directly; and he's lost flesh, one can see that at a glance. He's been working too hard, perhaps; and I don't like that sort of *hungry* look he's got; it's a bad sign; and he's no appetite, not a bit. I watched him at breakfast. He drank his tea eagerly, but he didn't touch a morsel of food. But I think I could soon put him right, if he'd let me. I could make him up a pill, to be taken at night——"

"I'm sorry we didn't keep him down in Wales," Cluny Puckle interrupts. "He was hearty enough there; but now he's very peakish-looking, certainly. He's as white and as lean as any Cockney of them all. But I never thought much good would come of his graving images up here in town. As for pills, Williams, no thank you; I say, a stiff tumbler or two of whiskey toddy, real Glenlivat, boiling hot, the last thing before he gets into bed."

The curate said nothing, though perhaps he too had a remedy to propose, and was bethinking him of a chapter or two in a certain Book, full of sure and exquisite consolation, which he would have had Noel read diligently, and devoutly lay to heart. He had watched the young man with tender, thoughtful eyes, and had assured himself that his old pupil's malady was of the mind rather than the body.

The lofty-mannered footman in Cumberland Crescent was not much given to emotion; prided himself rather upon his apathy, and non-liability to external influences. Yet even he was much perturbed when a knock at the door, very late at night, summoned him to admit his master, faint and trembling, leaning for support against one of the pillars of the portico.

"Help me into the library, Joseph. Is any one up?"

"Missus has retired, sir. Miss Clare is in the drawing-room."

"Tell her to come to me, at once," Mr. Gifford said, speaking with a sort of gasp.

It was with difficulty he could walk across the hall to the library. He sank into his easy chair, leaning back, panting for breath. Soon Clare was with him.

"What is the matter?" she inquired, anxiously, as she twined her arms round him. "You are not well, papa; you are quite cold."

"It is nothing, Clare; nothing; a little cramped and chilled, that's all. I hardly thought I should find you up, Clare."

"I could not go to bed until I had seen you. What is the matter? Tell me; have you had bad news—of—of Herbert? Have you *any* news of him?"

Not unnaturally she attributed Mr. Gifford's state of agitation to some new discovery touching the misconduct of his son. Of Herbert's unfortunate marriage she was well aware. The runaway had left behind him a letter addressed to Clare; it informed her in tolerably coherent terms of the rash step he purposed to take, beseeching her, his "dearest sister," as he called her, to do all in her power in the way of intercession on his behalf, to obtain Mr. Gifford's pardon, or at least his forbearance. Clare had not hesitated to undertake for Herbert's sake the painful duty imposed upon her. But Mr. Gifford had stopped her peremptorily at the outset; he declined all conversation with regard to Herbert's flight and clandestine marriage. The subject, therefore, had been a sealed one in the drawing-room. Not so in the kitchen, you may be sure, although there was not in that region much genuine information about the matter. Still, Mr. Herbert's absence had been canvassed freely enough; with a vivid appreciation of the mysterious and marvellous on the part of the lofty-mannered footman and his fellow domestics, that did them infinite credit.

"Yes, I can tell you now," said Mr. Gifford; "I knew before, but I wished to spare you. It little avails now, however. Herbert has brought shame upon us, as you know, Clare. He has fled, after contracting a disgraceful marriage; he is in Paris with his wife, the daughter of William Moyle, my discharged servant. He has brought shame upon us. Shame; yes, and worse than that, ruin!"

"Ruin?" cried Clare.

"Yes, Clare. He has committed a forgery upon the firm. He has given acceptances to a large amount, larger than at such a time as this

I can possibly hope to meet. But justice shall be done. The law shall take its course. It is due to my other creditors that this should be so. He must prepare to pay the penalty of his crime. He is no longer a son of mine. He has disobeyed me, and I cast him off. He is no more to me now than any other man who has committed an offence against justice. He has sinned, and he must suffer."

"No, no, papa; not so. You will be more merciful. You will spare him."

"It is not possible, Clare. It is due to others——"

"But I am rich, papa. I have a fortune; count it as yours, or Herbert's. Let it go to meet these forgeries, and spare him. Think how young he is. He has been the victim of others; he has fallen into some cruel snare. He would not have done this of himself, be sure he would not."

"My poor Clare," Mr. Gifford said, in a low, hoarse voice, "you have a noble heart; but this money of yours—can you bear to hear it? Indeed I did not mean to wrong you, but—it has gone with the rest; it has been swept away, involved in my misfortunes. The firm has stopped payment. Ruin has been impending some time.

Do what I could this was not to be averted. Pity me, Clare, if you can. *I am bankrupt!*"

And he covered his face with his cold, thin, shaking hands.

"I am bankrupt, Clare," he repeated; "and I have robbed you, my poor child, of everything that you possessed. All has gone."

She was silent for a moment, pale, frightened by his deep emotion, then she gently drew away his hands from his face, and kissed him, as she said in a low voice—

"You did rightly; it was yours, papa. If you had spoken a word, I should have given it up all to you. But there was no need to speak about it. Let it go. I wish it could have been of more service to you! I wish I had more to give you! Don't speak of this again. Don't think of it."

"You can pardon me, Clare?"

"Do not ask me. Do not think of asking me. You know I do."

"God bless you, Clare."

"But Herbert? You will not bring this dreadful charge against poor Herbert? You will be silent; you will not accuse your own son?"

He did not speak; indeed it seemed that he

could not. He was leaning back, with closed eyes, gasping for breath, with the waxen whiteness of death upon his face.

Clare was terribly alarmed; she rang the bell for assistance; for a moment she feared that he was dying. Presently, however, he rallied a little.

"My poor Clare," he said faintly, speaking with great difficulty, "whatever you may be told of me, whatever rumours you may hear, think as well of me as you can. Promise me you will. The world will raise its voice against me; will you be deaf to all that it may say? Try, Clare dearest, try, to think well of me always."

"Indeed, indeed, I will."

"Dear Clare, you have been as my own daughter to me. We have always been friends, Clare, haven't we? God bless you, Clare; you are a dear, good girl. God bless you, Clare."

He tried to raise her hand to his lips. He was not equal to the effort, however; a dead faintness came over him.

A doctor was at once sent for; but his presence gave Clare no great comfort. She read upon his face too sure evidence of anxiety and alarm. The patient was to be carried upstairs as gently and tenderly as could be to his bed-room on the second floor; yet even this order could not be wholly complied with. It was thought more prudent to stop half way at the drawing-room, and a bed was made up on Mrs. Gifford's sofa. The motion of the journey upstairs was more than the sufferer could bear. The least shock, one accidental jolt, and the pulsing of his poor, fluttering, aching heart might be stopped for ever. That piece of human mechanism was cruelly out of gear. He was insensible, yet still he breathed. Ever so feebly. His eyes were closed, his face was of an ashen grey, his lips, parted as though gasping for breath, were of a faint purple hue, his hands were stone cold, and his finger nails of a blue tinge.

The doctor could do nothing but prescribe extraordinary care. The patient was not to be disturbed in any way; was not to be spoken to or seen by any one; the house was to be kept as quiet as possible; no noise whatever was to be permitted; not so much as the loud closing of a door, or the creaking of a shoe; the knocker was to be tied up, and tan or straw laid down thickly in the street; all organs were to be sent away at any cost, and the neighbours were to be entreated not to play their pianos, and to stir their fires as gently as might be. In his present condition the very slightest excitement might be fatal to the invalid.

The night brought no change. Clare sat by the side of the sofa, wearily watching, speaking never a word, but now and then wiping the sufferer's clammy forehead with her handkerchief, or touching with a light caress his thin, cold, relaxed hands. The golden head was bowed beneath a deep sorrow. She had until quite recently lived so happily, had had so slight an experience of grief, that now the sunshine seemed to have gone from her path in life, and a dense cloud overshadowed it.

She had loved Richard Gifford. She had felt to him ever as a daughter to a father. He had been cold, distant, harsh even, to others, but not to her. From the first he had tendered homage to her beauty and her goodness. Disappointed in his son, Herbert, in his dullness, his vacillation, his feebleness of character, it indeed seemed as though Mr. Gifford had revenged himself in a way by the increase of his affection for Clare. He had thoroughly appreciated her. He had taken a pleasure in submitting himself almost absolutely to her will, in indulging ever her caprices, in abandoning even his wonted rigidity and sternness in her presence. This may have arisen from a sort of involuntary estimation of what was graceful and refined and elegant, or it may have been from a human longing to attach to himself, in spite of all the want of principle, tho selfishness, the shameful cruelty that had marked his career, the calm, strong affection of one good, pure Christian heart. He had sought to compound for much wrong done to others by the kindliness of his treatment of Clare. True, he had planned her marriage with Herbert; at one time he would possibly have sanctioned her union with Clement Buckhurst, convinced the while of his worthlessness. But he was inclined greatly to underrate the disadvantages of marriages which were the result of convenience rather than love; he deemed the reputed miseries of such unions a matter of sentimental exaggeration. He had been twice married himself; each time for interested and commercial motives, and had not been unhappy; and he had had an object to serve in procuring for Clare a husband who would have been of an accommodating nature; who would have made no very strict inquiries as to certain dealings with the trust monies in which she was interested, dealings which would not bear very close investigation. This was all altered now, however. The crash had come. Clare's fortune had disappeared for ever, drawn in and lost in the total wreck and sinking of the old established firm of Fordyce and Fordyce.

He had stood between her and Noel Tredgold. Never had he been so cruel to her as then. But could she remember this, when he lay beside her, senseless, dying; when perhaps from those pallid lips sound would never issue more? Could she now weigh this one act of severity against a life of kindness and indulgence, and pronounce against her step-father, withdrawing from him her love? It was not possible. She could now think only of how good he had ever been to her. For her loss of fortune, it was nothing; she had not given another thought to the thing. As yet perhaps she hardly knew what the phrase meant—loss of fortune—what was it to her? Hitherto she had been so prosperous and happy, that ruin and poverty seemed to be words without distinct meaning for her; at least it required time to bring them thoroughly home to her intelligence.

She loved Richard Gifford, therefore, and not niggardly: with no desire to think less tenderly of him. What he really was she knew not, did not care to know. To her he was as a fond father, and had a right to her best affection. She had given it, and would not take it away again. In the silent watches of the night she wept, and prayed for him. She had constituted herself his sole nurse, and the strict sentinel of his sick-room. Eager to hinder all interruption, to hush all noise, to do all that was possible to save a life that seemed to be hanging as by a thread.

The doctor came again on the morrow; still anxious and alarmed, it was plain. He began to shrink from the responsibility of his position as sole medical attendant; he suggested that further advice should be summoned, that indeed a consultation of physicians should be held. It was soon arranged that there should be a conclave of doctors to consider the condition of the invalid, and at three o'clock in the afternoon the back drawing-room was placed at the service of four eminent professors of the art of healing. Among these it so happened was Dr. Moxon, physician to the insurance company, in which Mr. Gifford held a policy he had endeavoured, ineffectually, to increase in amount.

The doctors contemplated their patient still stretched insensible upon the sofa.

Dr. Moxon saluted his professional brethren with a sort of hushed cheerfulness—a half-aside cordiality.

"I may as well tell you at once," he said, in a low voice, "that I have been admitted a little behind the scenes in this case. I saw our poor friend in the next room only a very few days ago. He came to me upon a little matter of business, in connection with a well-known insurance office, of which I have the honour of being the medical representative. I had occasion to submit him to a slight, a very slight examination. But I found mischief *here*" (he tapped his left side with a playful frequency), "very considerable mischief, I may say. I was not altogether unprepared, therefore, for the painful result we are now here to advise upon. I thought it prudent to caution our poor friend in a friendly way. I was not entitled to do more. He has never been a regular patient of mine; but I gave him a gentle caution against the ill effects that might ensue from his subjecting himself to excitement of any kind. I remember I advised him to withdraw from town, and not to trouble himself with business considerations of any kind. I think I recommended Dawlish, perfect rest, abstinence, sedatives, and depletion. It seemed to me that in these was his only chance. I fear our poor friend has really not acted judiciously. It is evident to me that he has permitted himself to be excited not inconsiderably; and he has attended to his affairs with unremitting devotion. It's very sad. What can we do when we are met, as we so constantly are met, with this unreflecting obstinacy in a patient? He has thrown over my counsels; he has been working hard, and exciting himself. I learn, indeed—for I was in the City this morning—that he has become bankrupt! Actually bankrupt, at this time of all others! Now, what can we do in a case of this kind—hypertrophy in the left ventricle, without a doubt. (Do you take snuff? It's a bad habit, but I'm too old now to leave it off, and I really think it's over-abused; I find it a pleasant stimulus, taken in moderation, especially in cases where the temperament is not of a sanguine or bilious character.) Yes, hypertrophy of the left ventricle. I am glad to find you agree with me. Our opinions, then, may be said to be identical. We must go on as we have begun. Extreme care must be used. We must strictly prohibit all influences having the slightest tendency to excite the patient. Time may do something, and I think, after another night, I may venture to say—eh?—that we had better meet again, and consider what is advisable to be done? Are we agreed upon that head also? Very well, then."

The consultation did not effect any very important results. But a consultation before a patient dies is as indispensable as a coffin after his death; and generally it may be about as much real consequence to him. Still both are tributes to decorum: and perhaps are sources of consolation and comfort to survivors. Death is robbed of half his sadness if he is preceded by "the best advice," and followed by "the completest of funerals."

The evening paper announced officially the suspension of the firm of Fordyce and Fordyce, with flattering mention of its antiquity, good repute, and a guess at the amount of its liabilities, and the probable dividend it would pay. No very great hopes, however, were held out in this last respect.

What did the bankruptcy, so much dreaded, so bravely, if unscrupulously fought against, matter now to the head of the firm, senseless upon the drawing-room sofa in Cumberland Crescent? What was the shame of failure? Nothing. Men might point, he could not see their insulting fingers; slander might whisper, he could not hear; his foes might triumph, but what was it to him now? He had no eyes to read the chronicle of his downfall in the "Money-Market and City Intelligence" of the evening paper. He was as one bleeding to death upon the field of battle—to whom victory or defeat are alike small matters.

He could not know, he could not feel his disgrace: hardly breathing, on the brink of the grave, and sliding downwards with how feeble a hold upon life! Messengers came up, post-haste, from the City, but they never reached him; letters and messages in great numbers—all stopped on the threshold by anxious, watchful, loving Sentinel Clare.

Mrs. Gifford had not left her room, overcome by the shock of her husband's illness, terribly frightened. It was better so. The poor, timid, crippled woman, could have been of no service downstairs. She was crying, but quietly, giving no trouble, sending an urgent entreaty now and then to Clare to be careful and not over-exert herself. She, poor lady, vain, weak, foolish, yet not altogether heartless, could play tolerably a part in the trivial, insipid, fashionable comedy of life; but when tragedy was to be enacted, when gloom and passion, sorrow and trouble were to occupy the scene, she was quite as well away from the stage. *En deshabille* in her dressing-room, too frightened even to screen her wrinkles from the light, or to hide her wanness behind cosmetics and rouge, she was very anxious to do what was right, and proper, and dutiful, under the circumstances. She learned with real pain of her husband's serious illness, though she had ever, perhaps, had more awe than affection for Mr. Gifford; but she was conscious of her own feebleness, while she had thorough faith in Clare's energy and cleverness; and greatly doubting, there can be no question, that she did altogether what was best—that is to say, she did nothing, keeping in her room quiet and miserable, interfering with no one.

There were many people coming to the door all through the day, rapping as noisily as the well-muffled knocker—it wore a thick poultice of kid glove—would permit them. The footman had his hands full; he affirmed that he never knew anything like it, not even in the height of the season in the houses of the most aristocratic of families. It was more than one person's work to answer the door; and the callers were insolent and pertinacious in their demands to see Mr. Gifford, indulging in brutal "chaff," when he was again and again denied to them. They wouldn't credit his illness: declaring it to be all "a plant" and "a swindle;" and that he was "keeping dark," and "out of the way," on purpose.

Poor Clare! It was cruel work for her. Echoes of altercations at the street-door could not but reach her, trembling lest her poor sufferer should be disturbed. Sometimes she would even herself descend to the hall to appease, as well as she could, the violence of the most persistent of the intruders.

There was no change in her patient; he still breathed ever so gently, but he had never spoken, never stirred.

"If he would say one word, but look into my face and know me, but press my hand ever so slightly!" poor Clare sighed.

Better as it was. Insensibility was more precious to him than consciousness. Why should he wake? To know the wreck of his ambition—the wretched futility of his life's struggles—to know that he had but risen in the world that his fall might be the heavier? Bankrupt, ruined, dishonoured; his Clare's fortune stolen from her shamefully, and gone with the rest; his son a fugitive, a forger, the husband of William Moyle's daughter; and Noel Tredgold demanding justice in the names of his dead father and mother, for all the infamous wrong-doing of the past! It were better to sleep for ever than to wake and know this.

Another urgent visitor, who will not take an answer: much to the irritation of the footman.

Noel Tredgold declares he will not quit the house until he has seen Richard Gifford. Clare quits her sentinel's post. Noel by her order is shown into the library. She joins him there presently.

"Dearest Clare, how long, how very long it seems since I have seen you!

"My own Noel, I am in such terrible trouble. Poor papa——"

"Ah!" and here his voice changes its tone. "It was to see him I came here. Let me not forget that."

"Dear Noel, it is not possible, he is so ill—so very ill."

"He is a villain!"

"Hush, hush, I must not hear you, Noel; you do not know what you say."

"Ah, Clare, if you knew what that man has done; the cruel wrong, the devilish wickedness!"

"Not a word," she interrupted; "he is to me as a father; he has ever been so; he is suffering painfully, and I love him!"

"You must not, you shall not, Clare; you cannot give your love to a monster like that—the merciless persecutor of my father and mother! It was he who brought ruin upon Bryan Tredgold—ruin, and exile, and death. It was he!"

"Noel, I can hear nothing of this now;" and she pressed her hands upon her ears to shut out the sound of his accusing voice. "What he may have done in the past can be nothing to me at such a time as this. If the whole world turn against him, I am bound to be on his side now. He has been ever kind to me. He is suffering—dying, perhaps; God knows! I will not leave him. I will not hear a word against him. He is to me only a father, who has need of all my love, my tenderest care; and he must have them; he shall have them."

She spoke with passionate energy.

"Do not seek to move me from my duty," she added; "do not, dearest Noel, I implore you."

"I, too, have a duty to perform, Clare," Noel answered, in a cold, calm tone; "a duty to the dead, which I will not, I dare not, leave undone. I must see Richard Gifford: the cause of terrible misery to me and mine. I must see him, and compel him to avow his own shame and my father's innocence! The truth has been hidden during long, long years. It shall come to light now, at last; by Heaven it shall! I should hate myself, Clare, if I could turn away and leave this unaccomplished."

She was very pale as she said, "Noel, you are without mercy."

"He showed none to Bryan Tredgold."

The tears dimmed her eyes as she took his hand and said, "But for *my* sake, Noel, for *my* sake, you will put away these revengeful thoughts?"

"Clare, you know I love you with my whole soul; do not ask this of me."

"Oh, as you value my love, Noel!"

"I *do* value your love, Clare; highly, very highly, Heaven knows; and yet there is a duty here I must not, I cannot shrink from."

"A duty!" There was both scorn and pity in her tone. She let fall his hand, and shrunk back from him with a look of despair.

"And you can abandon my love for this!"

"Clare, do not doubt me; do not drive me mad."

She was touched by the genuine passion of his manner. For a moment she paused; an inward struggle seemed to occupy her; she pressed her hands upon her forehead.

"I love him, I love him," she murmured piteously. "I cannot drive him from me; my heart will not let me."

She advanced to Noel again.

"Come then," she said sadly; "take your revenge, you merciless man!"

She led him upstairs, motioning him to tread as softly as possible. Soon they were standing by the side of Richard Gifford, pale as death, with closed eyes, senseless still, stretched upon the sofa in the drawing-room; and Noel looked once again upon the face of his father's foe.

The sight was a sad one: sad enough to soften a sterner heart than Noel Tredgold's. Gradually his thoughts of vengeance fled from him. Heaven had been beforehand with him. His enemy had obtained the sanctuary of sickness unto death. Richard Gifford was stricken down by God. Was there need of further blows from man? It could not be. Noel were less than man if he could think so.

No more of the human longing to repay blow for blow, and wrong for wrong; the Paganism of revenge was ousted from his breast. In its stead there came to reign a Christian pity and forgiveness. Did duty to Bryan's memory demand there should be outrage of that poor suffering, scarce animate clay? that insult and vengeful triumph should ring in the dying's ear as he sinks into the grave? And that higher duty due to Heaven, the pardon for all our trespasses, as we in turn forgive the poor mortal trespasses against us?

This the man who had triumphed over Bryan Tredgold; who had so prospered in the world; had gained such wealth and good repute? Well, he was brought low enough now. Death was at work, levelling all distinctions between him and his fellows. Richard Gifford's bitterest enemy might stand now by the side of his sick bed, and his enmity would abate and end for ever.

With softened heart and tearful eyes, Noel Tredgold turned away. Noiselessly he left the room, Clare gently following him.

"Clare," he said, "Can you ever forgive me? He has, indeed, need of all that human love and tenderness can do for him. Love him; tend him; pity him; pray for him. God forbid that I should hinder you, even in thought."

"My own Noel;" and she drew near to him with swimming eyes.

"You are an angel, Clare. I shall never be worthy of your love. Pardon me all I have said, dearest—the cruel pain I have caused you. *Can* you pardon me, Clare? *Can* you love me still, in spite of all?"

In a moment she was half swooning in his

arms, sobbing upon his breast, strained to his heart.

"It is hard to forgive, Noel; one of the hardest of all our trials here," said good David Griffith, the curate of Llanderych. He had learnt from John Moyle something of the young man's history—the past sufferings of his family. "It is hard to forgive: for human hearts are stubborn. But upon forgiven trespasses, be sure we mount, as upon steps, nearer and nearer to God's throne. To do right always, trusting in Heaven's justice, can a man have a nobler duty to perform? Believe me, our poor Bryan had never cause to be prouder of his son than when Noel Tredgold turned away and left his father's wrongs unavenged!"

A lingering through a few days: then the end. Take up the tan; unwind the bandages from the knocker. Richard Gifford is out of ear-shot now of the loudest human tumult. His aching, troubled heart is painless now; it has ceased to beat for ever. Bankrupt and dead, let his creditors do what they list with his estate, apportioning to themselves such dividends as they can. Let the claimants under the forgeries come in with the rest. There is no one now to say nay to their claims, and denounce the frauds committed by a son upon his father. Herbert Gifford is safe, so far. There may be suspicion; there can be no certainty. His chief accuser will not leave his grave to prosecute; and without his evidence there is no sufficient case against the culprit. Admit the forged bills with the genuine to their share in the very limited available assets; no one will be the wiser, and a terrible load will be off Herbert's heart—the fear of discovery; for the shame of sin—that is his for ever. Buy the bills, in fine, a thousand times over, and *that* will still remain, poor wretch! his eternal possession.

CHAPTER XII.

"CROWNER'S QUEST LAW," AND OTHER MATTERS.

A DOZEN men, with a thirteenth acting as chieftain, file into the accident ward of the Middlesex Hospital. Upon a narrow iron bed, hemmed in with screens, giving it a sort of dignified privacy and exclusive importance, lies the object of their visit. The coroner and his jury are holding inquest upon the body of William Moyle, late a patient of the hospital, brought in there on a shutter, the victim of a street accident, carried aloft in a sort of ghastly triumph, a crowd following: young and ragged, but excited and pitiful. The hospital's best skill and science are forthwith brought to bear upon the patient; how great that skill and science, how complete, humane, unceasing; how absolutely given to the sufferer, there is little need here to descant upon. Babylon may fairly take pride in its hospitals and their medical staffs—enlightened, unwearying almoners of healing. But human aid will avail little in this case. The accident was a bad one enough; yet all might have gone well with him if the man had not been for so long a time so persistently in training, as it were, for death. His vicious habits had reduced himself to a state of health that must have yielded under a much less serious mishap than this frightful cab-upset and run over. If the man had not been in such haste to meet his fate half way! "If he had not tampered with his constitution so terribly!" the medical staff justly exclaim, as they sponge and dress, splinter and bandage. He had been busy searing away his life hard as he could with liquid fire for some time past. So there was no help for it; Messrs. Fordyce and Fordyce's old, grey-headed, but not respected, not honest servant, went to meet his master, Richard Gifford, the head of the firm, in the grave.

The jury did not fancy their errand much; that was evident. Not that they ventured upon morosity or sulkiness; they had too much of Britannic respect for the majesty of the law, too much consciousness of the dignity of the official character they had been compelled to assume. It was a reputable thing to be on the jury; a tribute to their fair fame, worldly prosperity, and house-holding respectability. But it was an unpleasant duty nevertheless; the examination of the body especially. Yet there was no escape; it must all be gone through with, however perfunctorily. The jury took therefore, formal, brief, timid glances at the disfigured corpse upon the narrow iron bed—not a pleasing spectacle by any means. They made their examination as slight as might be; but it was quite enough to give them bad dreams for some nights to come. Many shop counters and desks, and back parlours, were haunted by unexpected memories of William Moyle's dead face long after the inquest.

The coroner certainly set them a strong example; shamed their weak nerves and feeble stomachs. He seemed to take a pride in manifesting the intimate, easy, hob-nobbing sort of terms upon which he stood with disease and death. He was thoroughly inured to the unpleasantness of his important functions. He was quite at home with the corpse. He paused in the midst of a particular (over particular, some of the jury thought) investigation of the body, to refresh himself with a pinch of snuff, without spilling a grain, or the slightest trembling of his fingers even. He constituted himself the guide and showman of the party, directing the jury's attention here and there, as though it were a mere wax-work chamber of horrors he was hired to exhibit—a curious mechanical piece of business, rather agreeable and attractive than otherwise—and not at all a poor fellow-being's body, crushed to death grievously. But then a coroner is bound to be diligent and clever and official, and above all, exhibition of feeling and custom must, more or less, engender callousness

There were other spectators also, it should be stated, who did not abandon their equanimity in any way, but were on the contrary charmingly collected and unembarrassed. I am not alluding to the beadle: simply because a beadle has never been known to disappoint legitimate expectation in these respects; but to the rather threadbare, tobacco-scented gentlemen, who, throughout the inquiry, in inconvenient situations and uncomfortable attitudes, were busy taking notes and preparing reports as representatives of the public press—the somewhat under-valued and over-ridiculed "liners," purveyors of much entertaining matter for perusal during breakfast hours; —who can boast perhaps a large majority of readers over more pretentious writers; who all follow their useful vocation zealously and reputably enough, though their literary style is not unimpeachable (whose is?), and their fondness for certain routine stereotyped forms of expression may be open to remark. But try, O pickers and choosers of words and artful builders of sentences, to prosecute your literary labours in a crowded court, a stifling atmosphere, with other men's elbows pressing into all parts of your frame, the top of a limp hat on your knees by way of a writing-desk, and the printing-press clamorous for copy, and let us see how perspicuous a chronicle of the events passing under your nose you can produce, and how admirable may be your dealing with the Queen's English!

The inquiry terminates at last. The jury find that the late William Moyle met his death by misadventure: being in a state of intoxication at the time; and censure the carelessness of the cabman, whose neglect of duty led to the accident. The censure will no doubt be conveyed to the cabman when he is in a likely state to comprehend it; at present he is by no means in such a condition. With a badly-broken head he occupies a bed in another part of the hospital, talkative enough, for he is delirious, and has been incapable of a sensible word or a lucid thought since the accident. By the time he is himself again —it will not be very soon—and has thoroughly digested the verdict of the jury, he will probably be sufficiently punished for a mischance which was hardly of his bringing about. As a cabman, who has constantly visited the hospital to ascertain the state of his afflicted fellow, puts the case: "Blow it all, you know, when a fare keeps on handing up a full glass to a cabby, what can he do but empty it, I should like to know? You would'nt have him chuck it away, would you? No: I should think not, indeed. Well, that's all poor Smithers done; and got his head jolly well broke in consequence; and him with a wife and family too! It's hard lines, that's what I say it is." There is unquestionable truth, it must be allowed, about cabby's view of the transaction.

The jury separate to recruit themselves with small glasses of brandy, and to return again to their normal occupations; now that the sad business is quite done with, rather pleased at and proud of it, and not loth to converse concerning their share in it. If nothing else, they are the richer by a new topic; and bating occasional apparitional memories of the dead man's face, they are not dissatisfied with the part they have played and the functions they have performed. There are many things not wholly pleasurable while in course of endurance which will yet bear to be looked back upon very tolerably, and in such wise, occasion indeed not inconsiderable comfort. Perhaps continental touring may be accounted among these matters.

The reporters send in their narratives, and the press soon sets up the MELANCHOLY OCCURRENCE, or FRIGHTFUL ACCIDENT, according as the fancy of the writer heads his paragraph, to be read by hundreds of thousands on the morrow. One of the readers being Mrs. Trinder, in the kitchen of John Moyle's house in Quebec Street; the time being night.

Mrs. Trinder, with an eye to the derelictions of her husband, thinks she may as well "improve the occasion," to borrow a pulpit phrase. She reads the report aloud. She was well informed of the facts of the case before; indeed she was in possession of more details concerning the victim of the accident than were at the service of the reporter, or than the newspaper authorities would permit him to make public. But still, to her thinking, *print* made such a difference! The affair was doubled in importance now that it could be read in a newspaper, like a murder, or a fire, or a revolution, or any other event of national interest. It was very nice to have a thorough previous acquaintance with the subject; but it was nicer still to be able to read her information set forth clearly in reporters' phrases, such as she would never have dreamt of employing, but which conveyed her own views so completely.

"They may well call it a 'melancholy occurrence,' for such I'm sure it is: and one we may all lay to heart. Not that I ever thought much of master's brother myself, Barty; a creepy-crawly, fuddled, dumb sort of an old man, he always seemed to me. But, there, poor soul, he's gone now where they don't set much store upon looks or manners either, I'm thinking. I hope you'll let it be a warning to you, Barty! 'The frequent and habitual recourse to ardent sperrits,' the newspaper speaks of. I should have said plain, 'a-drinking too much gin,' which is shorter; but very likely they both amount to the same thing in the end. That's how the accident came about, you may depend upon it, Barty; and if you don't take very good care, Barty, you'll go slipping off the hooks yourself, just in the same awful sudden sort of a way; sure as a gun you will. Down through a trap-door outside a public-house, which you didn't see was open; or backwards into an airy when you go leaning against the railings, taking for granted as the gates is locked, and often they is'nt; or full length in the middle of the road, and a 'bus over your poor legs, or one of them horrid Pickford wans over your chess before you can say Jack Robinson; that's what will happen to you, Barty; only see if it don't, unless you turn over a new leaf and mend your ways; and all along of drink."

Barty had been listening at first carelessly, chuckling, swaying about his head until his pendulous nose shook freely. But Mrs. Trinder, raising her voice as she went on, reached at last such a height of intense, solemn, menacing prophecy, that her husband was compelled to abandon his indifference, and to hint at some dim apologies that might be made for him.

"It's all very well talking, missus," he jerked out, "but a man must whet his whistle, you know; it stands to reason. If you was always getting plaster of Paris in your throat, or swallering marble-dust by spoonfuls, as I'm obliged to do, why *you'd* be wanting summat to wash it all down and freshen yerself up with, would'nt you? Of course you would. He took gin, did he?" And Barty looked meditative, smacking his lips, as though by an effort of thought he could conjure a juniper flavour on to them. "That killed him, did it? Well, I shan't die of gin, that's one comfort. I never get the chance; I can't afford it."

"But you drink beer; it comes to the same thing in the end, Barty," observed Mrs. Trinder sadly.

"Oh, does it! that's all you know about it. What's half-a-pint o' porter, or 'four ale'? *That* can't kill a man."

"Ah, half-pint after half-pint, and you may soon wash away the finest constitooshon in the world; and it's growing on you, Barty. You're nothing like the man what you were. You had'nt that red nose years ago, or I wouldn't have gone to church with you, you may take your oath of that, for no amount of money, I wouldn't. You must give it up, Barty; or something awful will happen, I know there will. I get *that* nervous now when you get stopping out, Lord knows where, that I can't set down or stand up for thinking about what's like to have befallen you; while as for going to bed it's a mockery, if it means getting a wink of sleep. And now see what's happened to master's brother, poor man; and how can you expect to fare better nor him? Of course you can't: but worse if anything, more likely—dying in a 'ospital with medical students sticking their knives into him, and cutting him up before he's half dead, to see what he's made of! I know their tricks; and that's what you'll come to, Barty, or worse. Take my word for it."

"There, there, don't fret, old woman, I'll mend; you see if I don't. Why, I'll take the pledge, if you like; there, I'll go out and take it now." (Apparently Barty considered it to be something medicinal purchaseable at the chemist's, and a certain specific for intemperate habits, to be taken whenever the complaint might be troublesome.)

"Now you don't, Barty; you don't go out of my sight again this mortal night," said Mrs. Trinder promptly, and she eyed her husband suspiciously. "I know about what your taking the pledge would come to. You can't deceive me, Barty; let you try never so. You'd have to step into a public-house to ask your way, you would; and by the time you stepped out again you'd have drowned all thought of what you'd been going to do, and you'd be too blind and muddled to go anywhere but into the gutter or the station-house along with a p'liceman each side of you, propping you up and shoving you along as though there was no more life in you than in a Guy Fawkes; and no more there ever is in a drunken man, except he's more noisy and worse behaved. I've seen guys that perfect as to figger, and expression, and dress, and sitting upright, that many a man, especially a husband, would do himself credit by a-striving to imitate 'em. If you don't make a change, Barty, depend upon it you'll come to a bad end, and there'll be a jury sitting on you, and a coroner asking all sorts of questions, and a beadle stalking about as if the whole place belonged to him, and reporters putting you in print, and doctors making mince-meat of you; that's what will happen. And what will master think of it all, I wonder? He won't be put out at all; no, I dare say not; not a bit; and what do you suppose *my* feelings will be? Your poor wife's—your widder I shall be then—that I should live to say the word! Sworn in by beadles and ushers, and giving evidence, dragged here, and druv there, bullied and bother'd about, and cross questioned—it would be the death of me, I know it would! And it ain't what a respectable woman ought to be made to undergo. But a lot *you* care! If I went on till I talked all the voice out of me, and had no more breath left in my body than in those old bellers there with the slit in them, *you* would'nt change! No; nor so much as give up one half-pint, you wouldn't! I know you; like all the men: as obstinate as master's marble images, only not so pleasant looking; any way they don't scowl when you talk to 'em, or give you black looks in change for kind words; and if they don't open their mouths to speak, why they don't open 'em to pour drink down their throats; there's *that* to be said for them. Bah! I hate a drunkard: and that's what you're getting to, Barty, as fast as fast can be, say and do all I will."

Mrs. Trinder did not stop here. She continued for some time her lecture upon intemperance—the floodgates of her eloquence once being loosed they were not easily closed again, as Barty found: as indeed he had often enough found on previous occasions. Like other enthusiastic orators she was much moved by her own harangue; and tears and sobs, and other symptoms of hysterical emotion came at last to hinder the progress of her speech. Barty's face assumed a penitential expression, and solemnly he promised amendment in the future. So he bought present peace. And here we will leave the Trinders. Let us trust the wife had no further occasion to complain of the husband. But the pledge is soon taken and soon broken. Mrs. Trinder, however, was not indisposed to a compromise. She would probably be satisfied with a reasonable diminution in the number of Barty's "half-pints." After all, it was but a poor sacrifice for a wife to ask; she ought to have obtained it even if she didn't.

John Moyle and Jemmy Stap had met at the inquest upon no unfriendly terms. Former misdoings of the young man in the studio of the sculptor were condoned, and the nephew was re-admitted to the confidence of his uncle.

"I think, Jemmy," said John Moyle, "we must get you to see after poor old grandfather, now William's gone. We must set you up in charge in Whitfield Street. I'll take care you're not a loser by it. As for Liz——"

"Not a word about her, please," Jemmy interrupts; "I don't think we've need to give her a thought. We shan't see her any more, you may be sure of that; she's cut the lot of us, she has; she won't show in Whitfield Street again; she won't bother herself about us; why should we bother ourselves about her? A thorough bad 'un, that's what she is; I didn't think so once, but I know it now for certain; and I don't want to hear so much as her name mentioned, never any more, I don't."

And Jemmy accepted the care of old Zachary,

taking up thenceforth his abode in the house in Whitfield Street, of which the late William Moyle had been lessee. It was a good thing that this employment was given to the young fellow; not so much because the flight and treachery of Liz Moyle had inflicted a wound upon his heart, to be healed upon by the effluxion of time—most simple yet most certain of remedies—but because some settled occupation had become necessary to him; it was most desirable that he should have a subject to reflect upon, something to which he might devote his energies after the cessation for the day of his duties to the Messrs. Gashford.

Bereft of the pastime of love-making, and rid of all demands upon his leisure in the shape of planning out his future married life, and bargaining for the household wares, which were to have decked and cheered it, his evening hours might have hung very heavily upon his hands; and the fascinations of "half-price," the bagatelle-board, the musical and the sporting public-house, might have exercised a baleful influence over him; he might have sunk into a quagmire of shabby dissipation and cheap and nasty viciousness, from which he would have found it difficult to emerge. The "frozen-out" lover may soon turn his compulsory lack of employment to bad account, and fling his self-respect and good repute and promise after his lost love. But Jemmy did not do this. He lamented a little his hard fate, and railed against the sex, as he had some title to do; but in the end he accepted his position manfully, determining to make the best of it. There was a strong substratum of good nature about his mental organization; he bestowed very kindly care upon his old grandfather, who, indeed, stood in need of such attention, growing more and more infirm and feeble every day; the childishness of second childhood now very strong upon him.

"My mind seems all of a buzz like," the old man would sometimes avow; "I don't think I remember things so well as I used to. What was that you told me about William the other day? Sure-ly, it does seem a long time since I seen his legs go by the airy railings; and John came all in black, looking for all the world like a parson; a bran new suit; he didn't use to be so fond of dress; I've known him look shabby enough. But I don't say nothing agin it. He's got money, plenty of money; let him spend it if he likes; he's been *near* with it, very *near* for a long, long time. Ah, he said William had gone away; yes, I remember now, gone away, and we should not see him again for ever so. Something to do with Fordyce and Fordyce, I shouldn't wonder; and along of things being queer in the city. They're a wonderful important firm, and they've got correspondents, and agencies, and that, all over the world; and William's their confidential clerk. I dare say he's gone travelling for them, or something of that sort. Ah, and there's Liz too——"

And then he would break off, rubbing his wrinkled old forehead with his lean palms in a futile effort to recollect what had happened to his granddaughter Liz.

He had been informed, in due course, of the death of his son, of the marriage of Liz. For a few minutes he had seemed to be greatly struck with the importance of the news. He had comprehended for a brief space that John Moyle was wearing deep mourning for the unfortunate victim of the cab accident; that Liz had eloped with Mr. Gifford's son, and that so far the dreams of her prospering in that respect had been really brought to pass. Yet very soon all recollection of these events had faded from his memory; his mind could receive an impression, but had no power to retain it, and presently it had faded, and gone as absolutely as writing from a quicksand; and he was asking whether William wouldn't soon be coming in from the City; and was looking out eagerly for his son's legs in their passage by the area-railings, or was wondering why Liz never now came rushing into the kitchen, shedding around pomatum-odours from her glossy curls, as with braceleted wrists and ringed fingers she bent over the kitchen fire, drawing hot water from the kettle on the hob. More and more, as time went on, his mind seemed "all of a buzz like," to use his own phrase. Perhaps it was better so. The poor old man was spared some pain very likely. He had few wants, and these were all carefully supplied. He had few pleasures; the programme of his life was reduced to very simple and slender proportions. To sit over the fire, toasting his knees, now dozing for hours and hours together, then waking up for a fit of garrulity, when he was perfectly content if there was some one by making believe to listen to him, nodding and smiling to him at intervals to affect an interest in him and his conversation. Basins of broth and sticks of dry toast, prepared for him with much punctuality; and a regular supply of that dry, ginger-looking snuff he most affected: he had few necessities out of this enumeration. And by and by he forgot all about his son William and his grand-daughter. His memory never being fed by the sight of them, went out like a lamp without oil. Next he was beginning to have doubts concerning the identity of his son John, confusing him in a strange way with the clergyman who came now and then to see him; with the doctor; with, indeed, some long-forgotten old employer of his, years ago, when he was little Zachary, a labourer's son, scaring away the birds with a rattle, far away among undulating fields and shady hedgerows in the country. He had some uncertainty, too, touching the identity of Jemmy Stap, yet sought to master this as much as possible—cognizant of his grandson's kindness, and taking a senile pleasure in patting the young fellow's hands now and then, or stroking his head caressingly. Very simple matters amused him greatly now. A comic song, executed by Jemmy—though the old man could not hear more than half of it, and could not comprehend that—or an impromptu performance of Punch and Judy with the aid of two forefingers and a knotted handkerchief, or the cat danced about by Nance, and made unwillingly to go through a sort of forced hornpipe—these occasioned him fits of mirth that seemed almost dangerous, they were so excessive. So old Zachary arrived at life's last scene of all: at second childishness, and mere oblivion; a sad enough state, for it announces the end, preludes death. Quite otherwise the imbecilities of infancy, the helplessness of first childhood. Who sorrows over these? —they are but the beginning, ushering in life, and may but conceal priceless germs of future hope and promise.

I am glad in bidding adieu to Jemmy Stap, to be able to give good news of him. Not that he is going to be married; but a man may be hopefully comfortable in a celibate state, and Mr. Stap is for the present inclined to regard the sex much as a burnt child the fire. He has resisted therefore very strenuously certain blandishments to which he was subjected, emanating from Miss Minns, dressmaker, residing very near to Whitfield Street. This lady has changed her views considerably in regard to her former friend, Liz Moyle; she is very severe upon Mrs. Herbert Gifford. She has been known to denounce her old companion as a "scheming minx," "a brazen-faced hussy," "a shameless hupstart," etc., and to hint that she had always entertained the gravest doubts concerning her propriety of conduct; though to do Miss Minns justice, she had been remarkably careful thitherto to keep these doubts to herself. Mr. Stap did not receive this abuse of his former love with much eagerness; Miss Minns did not in such wise recommend herself to his affection. He said simply he did not want to hear anything more about Liz, for good or bad, from Miss Minns or anybody else. So the dressmaker was discomforted; had to exercise her wiles elsewhere. And of late Jemmy has been a zealous attendant at certain Young Men's Evening Classes. He is bent upon self-improvement and self-help. John Moyle furthermore is coming to his assistance. There is a talk of a premium being paid to Messrs. Gashford, of Gray's Inn, and certain articles being executed between a member of the firm and a young fellow who entered their office as junior copying and general clerk. I don't see, for my part, why in certain paths of the profession Mr. Stap should not make as excellent an attorney as a good many who now appear on the roll, little to its adornment.

For Liz Moyle and her husband, (I prefer that method of mentioning the newly married pair—the lady was by so much the more important of the twain—to employing the more ordinary form which assigns priority to the male), for Liz Moyle and her husband, married clandestinely and eloped to Paris—they were tolerably happy at first; less happy than they expected to be very likely; but then nobody is ever so happy as he or she expected to be. As a general rule, people don't differ very much immediately after marriage, being bent earnestly upon making the best of the new state of things in which they find themselves: disposed to be resigned to the irremediable. Sir Peter Teazle was surely exaggerating when he spoke of a little tiff on the way to church, and a fair quarrel before the bells had done ringing, stating that he was nearly choked with gall during the honeymoon, and had lost all comfort in life before his friends had done wishing him joy; or else his was a very exceptional case. Amiability and good temper, witching smiles, graceful compliance, and genial submission, are in ordinary certain to be found amongst the bride's paraphernalia, though they may not be invariably the most lasting articles of the trousseau; and in fact there would seem to be in such cases a mutual understanding that disagreement is to be postponed as much as possible, and the determination "not to quarrel *yet*," or "until we get settled at home," preserves peace very respectably for some time. Once in their own home, of course there can be no reason why the happy couple should behave very differently to other couples, happy, or unhappy, as the case may be.

And then, to a quarrel, to a difference of opinion, even, two are necessary. If Liz had tried ever so, she couldn't have quarrelled with Herbert: he did not give her the chance. He yielded to her in everything, indulged her every caprice, humoured her to the top of her bent, laboured to anticipate her wishes, even her whims. He worshipped her, to the very ground she trod on, and the boots she employed in so doing. He never seemed to tire of doting on and admiring her; did not yield even to a natural disappointment when he found that her French was less available for continental purposes than he had hoped it might have been. His devotion was unremitting, unreasonable: but a woman can hardly find fault with an infatuation, however foolish, of which she is the sole object. He was weak and fatuous, with occasional fits of alarm as to the consequences of the misdeeds preceding his departure from London, and his father's wrath thereupon; and he was certainly not very amusing. But, in respect of these drawbacks, his absolute love and idolatry were amply compensative, and for a space Liz certainly liked him; loved him indeed, next to herself, better than any one else in the world; but then the interval between these two regards of hers was remarkable; her love for herself was so absorbing and enormous, that her love for Herbert was dwarfed to most diminutive proportions.

She had won the prize she had so toiled and schemed for. She had risen in the social scale; she was a lady now, the wife of the rich man's son; she had left Whitfield Street for ever behind her; she was *en route* for the parks, Cumberland Crescent, and the world of fashion. She had a lady's-maid now, to aid her in her toilette, and was not kind or considerate to that handmaiden, wreaking vengeance upon her, as it were, for long years of comfortless, solitary, unassisted, dressing. For her now the ablest Parisian *modiste*, the choicest perfumery, a handsome equipage, a box at the opera, an exquisite low dress—making great revelation of the glories of her neck and shoulders, with flowers plentifully grouped in the hair it had been an afternoon's work to gloss and arrange and decorate. Great admiration for her now also: not of the most genuine or refined kind, for it came from men only, who proclaimed her "a superb animal," as indeed she was. The women voted her vulgar, coarse, and ill-bred; detected a *demi-monde* air about her, and were not loth to publish that discovery; complained of her rolling her eyes about, of her insatiable vanity, of her gross appetite for praise. She was not discouraged, she let the women go, drawing the men closer round her throne; they were more amusing, and their admiration was very downright and whole, if not absolutely honest. Herbert grew a little bewildered; he was happy that his wife was happy; he was glad that she was admired, since it was so evident she was fond of admiration; and there was some tribute to the excellence of his choice in the crowd of worshippers that flocked to her. Yet he could not but hate these vassals who tendered their homage with a bold glancing effrontery, that had something contemptuous about it. In time he began to grow jealous. His wife encouraged these men too much, permitted them too great a licence, listened to whispers to which a wife's ear should have been deaf. His first half quarrel with Liz was in reference to this subject. He ventured to remonstrate timidly upon certain over-free and unguarded conduct of hers. She replied insolently enough; and poor Herbert was silenced, and miserable. His idol was not all such pure gold as he had fancied; that was his first approach to the discovery of the utter dross and rubbish of which she was in truth composed.

Liz's reign of triumph as a rich man's wife was but a brief one. She was only a Twelfth-Day sort of queen; and she was in a land famous for the deposition of sovereigns. News came of the crash: and her throne shook under her. The firm of Fordyce and Fordyce was hopelessly bankrupt; the head of the firm was prone on his death-bed. Liz did not need to look at Herbert's white, scared face to know that this was ruin irretrievable. She had planned and schemed so artfully, unceasingly—for what? To be the wife of a beggar. She wept, screamed, tore her lace with her teeth, looked ugly even, heeded not how she looked, what she said or did in the mad rage of her disappointment. Her passion knew no bounds. Herbert was requested to suit himself with apartments in some other hotel. The conduct of madame, it was stated, could not be tolerated. There were loud complaints against her on the part of the other residents in the house. Poor Herbert! he had never understood his wife. He was in dumb consternation while she tramped up and down the room, like a wild beast in a cage, raving at him, loading him with accusations as the cause of her misfortunes, loathing him. Loved him? No; she had never loved him, she announced, with cruel frankness; and words of bitter contempt, peals of insolent mocking hysteric laughter rung in his ears. It was a cruel waking out of his fatuous dream of love and happiness. And this woman, to win whom he had sinned so deeply, had brought such shame upon himself and his family, had sacrificed everything, this woman who spurned him so infamously, was his wife!

But there is no need to make long work of the story of the marriage of Herbert and Liz, and its sequel. It was a sad business; and I prefer to deal with it as briefly and lightly as I may. Respecting one chapter in the history of that union, I would refer the lover of detailed information, attractive only because of its detail—as miniatures of the very uncomely are precious solely because of their particularity, having no other charm or value—to certain chronicles of law-cases. A sufficiently full report of GIFFORD *v.* GIFFORD AND —— is to be found in the Divorce Court archives. Monotonous records, ever repetitive, telling of unhappy marriages, faithlessness, cruelty, wrong doing, human frailty, over and over again, in an endless jumble. The cases before the Lord Ordinary have a striking sort of family likeness; the court is as a hall of looking-glasses; one suit is crowded round by numberless reflections and imitations of itself. But the lady who the most often puts in an appearance before the judge is, I think, she who has married merely to walk in silk attire, and to have silver to spare: as Liz married, though she failed to gain her ends. Her union with Herbert was a civil contract merely; they were joined together as husband and wife by one officer of state, and they were sundered by another, but far more important, government functionary. They had entered into partnership, and the agreement between them became voidable by reason of the misdeeds, the breaches of engagement of which one member of the firm had been guilty. Herbert had come over to England for business purposes soon after his father's death. He returned to Paris to find irrefragable evidence of his wife's guilt. Presently she fled with a lover, taking with her every available article of value. Poor Herbert passed several months in a debtor's prison. Mrs. Gifford and her daughter with some difficulty found the means out of the wreck of their fortunes to obtain his release, and to furnish him with funds sufficient to procure a legal separation from his wife.

"She was a dreadful woman!" Herbert now freely confesses. He never mentions her name without a shiver. The affair of his marriage has been a great shock to him; he has been looking wretchedly ill, and is very nervous and weakly. Quite lately, a purse having been made for him, he has taken ship for Australia, partly with the view of seeking his fortune in a new colony, partly in hopes that the voyage may re-establish his shattered health. He went on board ship coughing terribly, what people call commonly a "churchyard cough." And a doubt was freely expressed by many bystanders, that when he passed out of sight of England's cliffs he would never look on land again.

For Liz, her name of course has been scratched from society's visiting lists; entered indeed in society's black books. But there is real silver, and there is albata plate. There is bread of best wheaten flour, and there are loaves of inferior material, known as "seconds." There is a real society, and there is an imitative article—an albata "seconds" society. This last is a body of some importance, is certainly numerous. Of late years its ranks have been recruited largely from English *divorcées* and worse. It has in private much struggling under disadvantages and disabilities; it takes revenge for these in the magnificence of its public manifestations. At the operas, concerts, flower-shows, races, in the parks and gardens, you will find this albata society in foremost places, brilliantly attired, hectic in its enjoyment, loud in its laugh, loud indeed in every way. Liz was welcomed by this society; those who have only lately abandoned good repute are always made much of by those who have given it up a long time ago; these last seem to think that they are somehow brought nearer to respectability by intercourse with one who is quite freshly quit of it. And it is a rule to *fêter* converts—or perverts, if you like the word better. Liz has been seen at home and abroad, apparently happy, always superb, indolent, insolent, selfish, vain, and worthless, surrounded by a crowd of admirers. How long will this last? Youth and beauty shout defiance at retributive justice. When these are gone ——. We will stop here, please. If you care to pursue the subject you can do so without aid from me. I will not sadden or soil my closing pages with further accounts of Liz. So here I bring my history of her to a close. You can go on if you will, landing her in a prosperous second marriage, or in terrible shame, and want, and suffering. The world affords precedents enough of both these endings to such a career as Liz Moyle's.

CHAPTER XIII.

LAST LOOKS.

The show over, it behoves the proprietor to go round, carefully snuffing out his candles. Over one of these I linger for a moment. A feeble bent wick, that has emitted but a feeble ray of light throughout the performance.

The first column of the *Times* announced one morning the decease of Clare Adelaide, the widow of the late Richard Gifford.

The little woman, with the long ringlets hanging down on each side of her small face, "like the ears of a Blenheim spaniel," was no more; surviving but a few months her husband's bankruptcy and death. She had had no experience of trouble, had no strength to endure; she gave way under her misfortunes, gradually sunk, and died. If she had never done much good in the world, she had as certainly never done much harm. She was too weak, and fragile, and helpless alike for either achievement. She had been little more than a lay-figure, very pretty to look at in her youth—a thing to hang dainty clothes upon, but not to be handled too roughly, for fear of breakage, and coming to pieces. The world cannot afford to sorrow much at losing its lay-figures—there is always a plenty of them about. Perhaps the most grievous fact about the death of Mr. Gifford was, that it gave poor Clare a new sorrow to bear, and she was already sad enough—had already suffered severely.

The same number of the *Times* contained another announcement, higher up in the column, among the Births;—"At Paris, Lady Beauflower, of a son."

"Clem Buckhurst's nose is put out of joint," said a lounger at the Alcibiades Club, reading out the line in question.

"Yes, it's a decided bowl-over for Clem," agreed another lounger, varying the idiom which proclaimed Clem's discomfiture by reason of the birth of an heir to the peerage. "I thought he stood to win once, when that boat upset, and the twins were drowned. But a man can't expect such a stroke of luck as that twice in his life."

Clem was no longer a member of the Alcibiades. The members of that admirable institution forfeit their membership on becoming bankrupt or insolvent; and Clem had lately obtained release from prison by taking the benefit of the Act. The Commissioner, who had dealt very leniently with him, was inclined to be hard upon the creditors. He said that if tradesmen persisted in giving unlimited credit to young gentlemen of fashion, without proper inquiry as to their means, or securing themselves in any way, they must reasonably take the consequences of their folly. It was absurd to come to that Court with opposition when it was too late, the mischief having been entirely of their own creating. The insolvent was discharged.

Not to be received into favour again by his uncle, the Honourable Alfred Buckhurst, however.

"My nephew is an infernal scoundrel, sir," the colonel has been heard to declaim passionately, his face an alarming scarlet; "an infernal scoundrel. I beg you will never again mention his name in my presence." The colonel spoke with a severe and menacing air; he was not a man to be trifled with.

Clem made some unsuccessful efforts to approach the colonel, and then, conscious of their futility, had abandoned these for a line of uncompromising opposition; trying to have it understood that he had given up his uncle—Old Alf had grown to be such a proser,and bore, and fogey, not that he had been himself abandoned by the elder gentleman. It was at one time a sort of amusement at the Alcibiades—for at all clubs, especially it may be noted at that chief though least exclusive one, the House of Commons, very small matters yield a large crop of entertainment—in the kingdom of the blind the one-eyed is king, in the regions of dulness a very stupid jest is immensely applauded—it was a sort of amusement, I say, to watch from the club window the uncle and the nephew promenading separately up and down St. James's Street on fine afternoons, cutting each other dead every five minutes at their point of encounter. But it was agreed on all hands that Clem was not looking by any means the better for his incarceration and passage through the Court. The once delicate complexion had assumed a pasty, sallow, unwholesome tinge; his figure had lost its former graceful outline, had swollen to a grosser, coarser contour; and, either from lack of means to be careful concerning his toilet, or from a wearing away in his prisonment among unappreciative associates of his old refined skill and taste in dress and other matters, his appearance was now much less in his favour than formerly. It was not merely that he was now careless and slovenly; his former friends, eyeing him from the Club window, voted him to be decidedly "raffish." There was a look about him, they agreed, as of "a bad style of man." Yes, an awful verdict to that effect was pronounced against Clement Buckhurst by the authorities at the Club windows, who sit in judgment on the affairs of the world. It became the right thing to have no dealings whatever with Clem—to give him up entirely. He became that utterly hopeless object the colonel had discoursed upon, warningly, at a much earlier period of this history; a man who is "hard hit," and who announces that he is so by his bad hat, his soiled gloves—a London swell at his *nadir*.

At last he disappeared from London, to turn up at odd places on the Continent—a sponge, and fortune-hunter, with great skill at pool, and suspiciously good fortune at all games of cards. He was assisted often by his mother the Dowager, and his half-brother Lord Beauflower, repaying their kindnesses always by the most shameless ingratitude; for, in truth, he was not one whom it was of any avail to assist. He seemed to be fairly past amendment, or hope of it. He was to be heard of now and then attaching himself to such simple middle-class travellers, who knew nothing of his history, and thought it a fine thing to be in the company of an honourable, a sprig of the nobility, during their sojourn abroad. But even these find him out in time, and get quit of him, or he gets what he can from them, and vanishes. Should my readers, on their vacation tour, encounter Clem Buckhurst, they will know that it is not advisable to admit him to too close an intimacy; above all, they will not sit down to cards with him, unless they are prepared to play a very costly game. He, too, is well known in the "albata" society of which mention has been recently made, and which flourishes abroad not less than at home. More than once he has fallen in with Liz Moyle. Their meeting was very frank and cheerful. There is a sort of freemasonry binding together people of damaged reputations; it is only by union they can defy their common enemy, Respectability. Clem and Liz indulged in not very kindly mirth over the ill fortunes of their victim, Herbert Gifford. I mention this that the reader may the better appreciate the depth of degradation to which both had sunk.

Clem's race is not yet run. He is the wreck of his former self; only a small balance remains to him of his only original capital—his good looks, and his pleasant manners. He may end his days in a foreign gaol, a prisoner for debt, if for nothing else; or he may bleed out his life in a duel, following some of his exploits at *écarté;* or he may secure to himself comfort in his age by marriage with some tradesman's widow, with more money and vanity than discretion. Should this last come to pass, let us hope the poor woman may tie up her funds in a very strict settlement, for gold runs through Clem's fingers like water through a sieve, and, her property squandered, she could not count upon very kind treatment for long afterwards.

Mr. Cluny Puckle, I learn, has been prospering in Sardinia. He has saved money it seems, and has himself undertaken a small portion of the contract for the new railway, by which he reckons to realize a considerable sum. Though his beginning is a humble one, there is no reason why his ultimate success in this direction should not keep pace with the good fortune of other railway contractors. Mr. Puckle is very clever, shrewd, and prudent, with a sharp North British eye to the main chance. He is a man one might pretty safely back to win in the long-run.

"Curate Griff" still labours earnestly in Llanderych, and not in vain; for earnest, honest labour is never wholly wasted, though its results may not be immediately apparent. You may be tilling a hard, stubborn, dull soil, almost hopelessly, for the progress you make is very slight, the effects of your work very poor; but go on, the ground will yield in time; obstinacy can be overcome by a greater obstinacy.

He has been but once in London since he made his first appearance in that city with two other excursionists.

He came up to perform an important ceremony: to unite the hands of Noel Tredgold and Clare Gray. A quiet wedding enough; the bride putting off for one day only the crape she was wearing for her mother and her stepfather. Then a calm, sober, yet very happy honeymoon passed amongst the Welsh hills and vales. In the course of their journey the husband and wife travelled over the line of a railway company that has obtained some share of notice in this narrative, and is now mentioned for the last time. And they stood by the side of a grave in Llanderych churchyard, where a tombstone recorded simply that one Bryan, a gauger, had met his death by accident. Sorrowfully, solemnly they bent over the last resting-place of Noel's father, drawing nearer together, feeling their loneliness more as they thought how he had been taken away from them, how cruelly he had suffered, how nobly he had endured.

"Dear father and friend," said Noel, softly, "oh that you could witness and share our happiness; that you could see and love my Clare—my wife; that I could hear your lips pronounce a blessing upon our marriage!"

"He is in heaven, Noel, watching over, and loving us ever. Let us live so that in God's own time we may join him—never to part!"

A few last words before I put away my pen, closing this imperfect chronicle.

Some years have rolled away. We will look once again into that studio in Quebec Street, with which the reader, unless he have an unreasonable affection for studios, as I own I have, must by this time be almost too well acquainted.

John Moyle is alone, much older-looking, paler, thinner than formerly. His hands tremble, and his back is bent. He is contemplating a noble work in marble, a public tribute to one of England's worthies, his last achievement. (It was an exceptional performance, it must be understood; for Britain, with the best intentions in the world, has scarcely been uniformly successful in her monuments of the illustrious dead.)

For a long time the sculptor stands as though cross-examining the result of many months' anxious toil. Then he presses his hands upon his eyes.

"It will do," he says simply. And then after awhile he adds, "So I make an end. It's something to know when to stop. There's been laughing enough at artists in their dotage. They shan't laugh at *me*. Let them laugh at *that* if they dare." (He points to the statue.) "I have not done all I wanted—all I hoped to do. Who ever does? But I'll stop now. That's a good thing to leave off at. It might have been better. I know that. It should have been better; only poor Sculpture is in a cleft stick. Nudity is indecent nowadays: and dress is hideous. Yes, it's time I put away my chisel. Henceforth mankind has only need of masons; it's over with the sculptors. At any rate I've finished."

Soon afterwards he went out, walking slowly, leaving London behind him.

He made his way to a pleasant river-side house, far enough away from town to be amongst green fields, shadowed by trees, alive with birds, yet near enough to see Babylon a sooty cloud on the horizon. It was Noel's home. John Moyle entered the studio of his pupil, glancing round him at its contents. These were worthy of attention.

"I have been very vain, and selfish, and foolish," he said gently, humbly. "I may stop, but the world goes on ever. I come to an end, but a nobler artist has more than begun. Still I shall have some claims to man's remembrance and gratitude. Surely they won't forget that your first lessons, Noel, were learnt in my studio."

"You are pale and faint, old friend. You have been growing sad again. Why will you so seldom let us see you?"

"Dear Noel, you bade me make my home here some time ago now. I refused. I shrunk from the sight of your happiness, from some morbid feeling I find it hard to account for; but it seemed to me I had no right to try and share in your life, only to shadow it perhaps. I thought it better to struggle on alone in my own old way. I dreaded, too, a change in my method of life. I was cowardly about risking even so poor a matter. I have been a coward always; but I think differently now. I have finished work for ever.

My hand trembles, betrays me. My sight is failing. I can do no more. All I have in the world will be yours, Noel, and your children's; and I have toiled hard, and saved and spared, too carefully perhaps. Only let me stay here now with you, Noel, pottering about in the studio a little now and then, but doing no harm. I can't live alone now when my work's over. May this be so, Noel?" He spoke in broken feeble agitated tones.

"Surely it may. Haven't we begged of you that this might be over and over again, though you wouldn't listen to us?"

"You are very kind to me. And Clare, will she let me stay here?"

"Of course she will. You wrong her asking the question." Clare had entered the studio and answered for herself, greeting the old man with kindest smiles. In her arms she held a little girl with floss silk hair, hiding a round pink face in Clare's white neck, playing at timidity.

Crowned with maternity Clare shone with new and addod beauty.

"You must never leave us again," she said to the old man. "You must make your home here," and she pressed his hand. "Believe that we will do all we can to make you happy: we who owe so much to you."

"Don't speak of that," he said, hoarsely.

The child in her arms here changed its mind about being shy and bashful, opened wide its blue eyes, clapping its tiny palms together, uttering a crow of baby triumph and welcome.

"Will the little one come to me?" John Moyle asked, watching the child with a curious interest.

Baby was a picture of "goodness," behaved exemplarily, permitted herself to be deposited in the old man's arms, nestling cosily there, without so much as hinting an objection; made herself on the instant quite at home and comfortable in her new situation.

"What have you christened her?" he asked of Noel.

"Ann."

They were silent for some minutes.

"Yes," said the old man, with a strange tremulousness, his eyes dimmed now by his tears. "I will stay here. My home shall be here."

"We will be as your children," said Clare, tenderly; "and baby shall be your grandchild. Give her to me again if she is troublesome."

But the child had sunk to sleep in his arms, and the old man would not let her be disturbed.

THE END.

CPSIA information can be obtained
at www.ICGtesting.com
Printed in the USA
LVHW040026180422
716440LV00005B/399

9 783752 595369